THE RIVE

By John McGauley

MW01152874

CHAPTER 1

THE BODY

We were in a backwater, Lucy and me, when we found the body. That was way back when we were crazy about each other and every night was supercharged with the raw, powerful voltage of love and lust. I was never again to feel such intensity about life but later realized that you couldn't live that way for long because you'd burn yourself up with muscle, hormones and hopes. I think a lot of people experience a time in life like that and think back about it with fondness when they're older and life didn't work out quite the way they thought it would.

The propeller on the little six-horsepower motor of the johnboat got tangled on something in the slough we were in a bit north of Quincy on the Mississippi River. That's what they call the backwaters of the river up where I grew up in Illinois, a slough, pronounced "slew." When the boat stopped the heat and humidity caught up with us, our bodies instantly glistening with sweat. Soon the mosquitoes would find us. You don't want to be stalled out in the sloughs for very long as swarms of insects were just waiting to make your life miserable. When that happens nothing helps, there's no repellent you can put on that keeps them off your body.

I dropped my hand down into the water next to the jammed propeller. Stuff in the slough was always wrapping itself around them. That was nothing new. Lucy sat up front, so sexy and pretty in that swimsuit that just looking at her got me all excited. I just wanted to be near her all the time and pretty sure she felt the same way.

Whatever was wrapped around the propeller wasn't going to be easy to remove. It felt like rope or maybe heavy fishing line. I thought maybe I could just cut it with my knife. Ever since I was a teenager I've carried around a small pocket knife and it always surprises me how often I've needed it.

"I gotta go in the water, get this thing untangled," I told Lucy. "This should just take a minute and we'll be out of here."

I slowly edged over the side of the boat and eased into the murky water. You never wanted to jump into the waters of a slough, never knew what was below. Logs, maybe even an old car or a sunken boat. Not that people dump stuff there, but because the Mississippi is so powerful during flood season it can transport anything caught in its path, drop it miles downriver. My buddy Louis had slashed his calf wide open when he hit an old rusted oil drum up near Canton last summer. We had a hell of a time trying to stop the bleeding and get him to the hospital. I had wrapped a towel tight around his leg and cinched it with a drawstring from my swim suit. He fainted twice and I had to slap him a couple of times to bring him back. A year later he still didn't walk right but the doctors told him that eventually he would. It was too bad because Lou was one of the best athletes around and this ended his chance at a baseball scholarship to Western Illinois University.

It was probably four feet deep where I went in. I had old tennis shoes on because again you don't want to step on some of the shit lying at the bottom. I could feel my feet sink into the soft mud, the water cool, refreshing, the weak current coursing past my torso. Of course in the main channel of the Mississippi that current is ten, twenty times stronger and there's no use fighting it, just go with it, slowly swimming your way to shore. Don't ever panic in that river, many people have lost their lives fighting it. When my dad was a kid he told us that he'd lost a friend in the river. They didn't find his body until nearly Thanksgiving, when some fishermen down near the lock and dam at Quincy pulled up some remains when they were trolling for carp. That kid had left his house one afternoon and nobody saw him again till they pulled his remains from the water, my dad said.

I felt the blades of the propeller. Some kind of rope had wrapped itself around it a few times. Lots of ropes like this are in the river, mostly from anchor lines that get loose, tie-ups that fall in the water from docks, abandoned trot lines. Hell, this one could have been from a couple hundred miles upriver, Davenport or even Dubuque. It was the plastic kind, the worst because they never disintegrate and they're a bitch to untangle. It was slippery with goo moss like everything else that spends time in the river. The Mississippi is really dirty and although we spent a lot of time there I guess you could think of it as a really big sewer. The water is rarely clear, that's why it's called the Muddy Mississippi. I learned later that the word for cloudy water is turbidity, a term used by hydrologists. For some strange reason I've always liked that word, and it often explains a lot of situations in life.

The rope felt like it was long, sunk deep and far behind the boat. I got a grip on the rope, pulled myself and it back on board with Lucy's help. Once there I could cut it with my knife, but for some reason I didn't do that right away. I pulled on it, curious about what it may be secured to down on the bottom. All kinds of weird things were in this river and I wanted to see to what that rope was attached. There's a natural attraction to see what's on the end of stray ropes in the river, never quite sure what you'll bring up to the surface. A couple of years before I was in a fishing tournament and I pulled up what I thought was probably a nice-sized catfish. It had a lot of fight to it but when I pulled it to the surface and into a net it turned out to be a woman's purse. The reason it felt like it was fighting was it was being turned every which way by the current as I brought it up. There wasn't any money inside the purse, just some Polaroid snapshots, dim images too waterlogged to make out what they were of. Probably fell out of a boat somewhere.

This rope wasn't hard to reel in, so it wasn't stuck on anything big or heavy, maybe branches or a small log. Sometimes these ropes were tied to cinderblocks, used by some boaters as crude anchors. If they couldn't pull them up they'd just cut the lines, go on their way, get another cinderblock. Those are hard to pull up, but this rope had give, attached to something but not too heavy that you couldn't pull it slowly toward the boat. It was a really long rope and I just kept pulling and pulling.

As I pulled it closer I could see something just below the surface of the water but back in the sloughs you couldn't see anything clearly until it was right on you. At first I thought it was a big old catfish, belly up and dead, a victim of an abandoned trot line. It looked bigger than any catfish I'd seen before and didn't have the right coloring for one of them, even a dead one.

When I saw the empty eye sockets I knew what it was. It scared the hell out of me, Lucy too because she was right behind me. I let go of the rope for just a second, the corpse slowly submerging a foot or so back into the water. Lucy screamed. I'd never seen a dead body before outside of a funeral home. Fish had eaten out the eyes, the body bloated, and the limbs stiff, akimbo. Strands of water grass were coming up with the body. It must have been held down on the bottom by the river grass. It looked like a big misshapen balloon, slowly rolling over once, like it was still alive.

This was in the days before cell phones, so it took us the better part of the day to get the police. I cut the rope and tied the part that held the body to a tree. There's no shoreline in a slough as such, just water blending into swamp at the treelines. I managed to untangle the other part of the rope from the propeller, started the motor and we made it to Hogback Island on the river where there's always some big powerboats tied up and people drinking and partying. We told them what we'd found and one of them went into Quincy and got the police. About two hours later Lucy and I escorted a police johnboat up to the place where the body was tied. They untied the rope from the tree and with wet suits on got into the water and hauled the body up into their boat. It was quite a struggle, heaving the body into their big police johnboat. They covered it with a tarp, took our statements and motored off. It was obvious these guys had done this many times before, it didn't seem to faze them. But they weren't cavalier about it either and in fact I thought they treated the body with respect.

They never did identify the body, but an autopsy showed there was probably no foul play involved, just a drowning upriver somewhere. Could have even been a suicide. Those things happened with some regularity on that river. It couldn't have been in the river long, though, since the body was relatively intact. One of the cops told me that it was probably there only two weeks, that the fish like to eat out the eyes first. A month in the water and there wouldn't have been much to retrieve, the cop said. Two months in the water and there wouldn't have been anything to find, he said.

It was just a blip in our summer. When you're that age you're not ruminating about life, not chewing it over as you do in later years when things become more calcified, and your future narrows, constricts. You live both in the moment and in the unlimited opportunities in front of you. One moment I knew Lucy and I would always be together – how could love like this ever end – and a moment later I knew I was going to leave Carthage forever and do great things. Of course Lucy would be with me, never thought otherwise.

How blissfully ignorant you are then, but it's both the best and worst thing about life that you can't know the future, can't even know what's going to happen the next day, or the next hour. We thought finding the body was exciting and upsetting and fascinating, but not life-changing. Only years later when I looked back at my life, and at Lucy's too, did I realize that the body represented our lives and what can happen when forces way beyond your control sweep you away in their currents. Blessed are the young and ignorant.

CHAPTER 2

JACK LAPOINT

He gazed out the window of his office high in the Prudential Tower in Boston, not really focusing on anything in particular. Raindrops smashed against the windows. Another dreary day. He looked down at his calendar – he still used an old-fashioned day planner – and saw that he had the morning clear of appointments and phone calls. Good. He was tired, up most of the night for no particular reason, just couldn't sleep. It happened occasionally, the sleeplessness. Nothing in particular was bothering him, it was just a vague feeling of uneasiness that had been coming over him for the last couple of months, that something wasn't right. It wasn't depression, or anxiety, but a nagging little notion there was something hanging over his head, ready to drop.

Whatever was bothering him was just short of serious enough to do something about it. He could live with it. Maybe it was just what growing older was all about. The feeling was strongest upon awakening, and ebbed throughout the day to the point where it wasn't even there by the afternoon when he usually was at his busiest. Then the next morning it would be there again and the cycle would repeat itself. He'd look in the bathroom mirror and see it in his face every morning. Jack LaPoint, once of Carthage, Illinois, and now a big-time attorney in Boston.

Otherwise, things were going pretty well. "Pretty well" meant that the law firm was firing on all cylinders and money was pouring in. When he'd arrived in Boston twenty-eight years ago he didn't have a pot to piss in, or a window to throw it out of, as the Boston Irish said. He'd been hired by a downtown law firm to do corporate tax work and the salary was pitiful, forcing him to rent a one-room efficiency in threadbare Chelsea, sharing a wall with a couple of wannabe mafia types his own age who supported themselves with a wide portfolio of petty crimes. The apartment was a dingy place furnished with junk, the kind of dump that's been painted over and over a hundred times and the bathroom shower can only spit out dribbles of water. You can get used to anything but shitty showers were the worst, you never grow accustomed to that. Later when he could afford a much better place he insisted that the shower be top-of-the-line, with new nozzles that sprayed as much water as possible.

It turned out he got to know those two guys next door pretty well, drinking beer with them on their back porch during the summer. The apartments were so close to Logan Airport they'd have to suspend their conversations while jets flew just 300 feet above, so close they could read the manufacturers' names on the engines. Every once in a while the three of them would go out to a local tavern called The Blue Goose and they would introduce Jack to some of their friends, the kind of people Jack had never been around in his protected life – Irish and Italian guys who were raised in the poor sections of Boston, none of whom had ever thought about going to college and supplemented their incomes with petty crime. Still, they weren't that different from any group of young people, just following different career paths. Their careers, though, didn't require nice downtown offices or suits and ties.

One of these neighbor guys was charged with theft and asked Jack to represent him in court. "I can't pay you right now, but when I score some money you'll be the first on the list," he told Jack. It wasn't a really serious charge, more like a glorified misdemeanor. On a lark Jack took the case, working on the side. Even though it was a small case it was much more interesting work than the soul-destroying boredom of corporate tax law. He was able to secure a dropped charge for the guy, one Cornelius Bonomono, a burly likeable Italian who made a living as a worker in an auto parts warehouse but on the side was a petty thief and sometime enforcer for a loan shark although he claimed he didn't like to hurt people. Jack couldn't envision Cornelius as an enforcer type, he was just too convivial, too many people liked Bonomono for him to be a real tough guy.

Then Bonomono's roommate, Lawrence Olivetti, got into trouble with the law, and this was a much more serious charge, assault with a deadly weapon. Olivetti had beaten the shit out of a guy using the kind of small baseball bat you buy at a concession stand at Fenway Park. This was a much harder case and it looked like it was headed to a jury. Jack spent much more time on it and had to come up with excuses at work to explain his absences. One of the partners at his firm saw him at the courthouse one day and asked what he was doing there since he'd called in sick. "Come to my office tomorrow," the partner told him. The next day he was fired and Jack had nowhere to go and no good prospects, not even a reference from the firm. He was in a stupor for three days, unable to rouse himself from his tiny apartment. There was no way he was going back to Illinois a failure, he'd find a way to get another job and stay in Boston.

He'd never forget the meeting at which he was fired. They brought him into the office conference room as if he were a prisoner in handcuffs, three partners arrayed on the other side of the table, all solemn like funeral directors. Only one of the partners spoke, a young guy named Stillwater who dripped with entitlement. "Mr. LaPoint, you've violated our rules, and I'm afraid you have to go," he said, Jack recalled, as if the statement were read by a British judge with wig and robe. "You'll be shown out immediately," he was told. And he was thrown out immediately, tossed out onto Beacon Hill on a snowy, shitty day. He walked around in that snow for hours, his nice shoes ruined and his mind a blur. Years later Jack would be in a similar conference room with Mr. Stillwater, but under very different circumstances. Like his mother used to say, life is long.

Jack was able to get Larry Olivetti off on the assault charge, but he felt different about Olivetti than he did about Cornelius. He thought Larry was a dangerous guy, somebody whose temper might be deadly. Once he said something to Larry and he took it the wrong way and Jack saw the anger flash in his eyes, and he saw in that moment that Larry might be a killer at heart, certainly crazy. Jack never felt comfortable around men who had bad tempers, and he had a sixth sense and could pick up slight vibrations about whether or not a guy had a volatile nature even before he showed it. He thought that the two roommates next door were mismatched, and couldn't figure out the chemistry between them. Maybe it was only because they were both Italian and had grown up in the same neighborhood.

As luck would have it one thing led to another and within a year enough of Chelsea's miscreants were hiring him that he was able to hang a shingle of his own, working out of a storefront next to a meat wholesaler in Chelsea. LaPoint and LaPoint it was called, although there was only one LaPoint. The place reeked from the smell of meat, he had no secretary, owned only a few desks and filing cabinets and used the copier down the street at a taxi-cab company. He had two suits, lived in the same shitty apartment and drove an old Toyota Camry with a hole in the trunk where thieves had hammered through the lock, stealing his spare tire. He kept the trunk closed with a bungee cord. He was 29 years old, single, and barely making ends meet. But he was having the time of his life being his own man, eating what he killed and rubbing shoulders with a huge ensemble of Boston's finest characters. Maybe it wasn't the kind of firm that's very far up the status ladder, but it was all his own.

In the years since then his firm had grown into one of the best criminal defense law firms in the city. That's saying something in Boston since half the city's population is engaged in one form of chicanery or another. He had a photograph of Cornelius Bonomono on his office wall to remind him of his humble beginnings. Whenever anyone asked him who it was, Jack explained: "That's the guy who started the firm with me." They'd stare at the photograph and wonder how a big guy in check pants and plaid shirt could have started such a firm. A lot of lawyers in Boston thought Cornelius Bonomono had actually been a founding partner of the firm. He still saw Cornelius from time to time, and the two of them had a special bond, although Cornelius was no longer a client. They always met at the same restaurant down in the harbor district and they always ordered the same thing – draft beer and fish and chips.

Cornelius had a son, Tony, who was now a law student at Suffolk University. "I want him to follow in your footsteps," Cornelius had told Jack during one of their lunches. It was ironic that his son had chosen law as a prospective vocation since Cornelius was connected with the mobs which operated in Boston. Jack never pried into Bonomono's business, and vice versa. The two kept their professional lives separate, their friendship rested on a mutual trust gained years ago when they were both just young guys on the upward trajectories of their respective careers. Between the two of them they knew just about anybody who was anybody on both sides of the law in Boston.

Occasionally LaPoint would drive by the old section of Chelsea where his first office had been but the building had been torn down and replaced by an upscale condominium project. The meat wholesaler and taxi-cab companies were gone, too. Chelsea was undergoing gentrification, as most of the old neighborhoods in Boston were and it was losing all of its color and smells. He always grinned when he saw the space where his office had been, recalling some of the characters who flowed through that place, all innocent victims of the criminal justice system, of course. Those were the fun days.

The name of his firm had been changed, and now occupied a suite in the Pru, as the Prudential Tower was referred to by older Bostonians, overlooking the city and harbor -- LaPoint, Maguire and Stockwell, with a dozen attorneys ensconced in plush offices. The clientele had improved considerably since the Chelsea days, they were just richer defendants who wore much better clothes and didn't commit crimes like breaking legs or selling crack, more like embezzling, insider trading, Ponzi schemes, every once in a while rape or murder. Same kind of people only with bigger checkbooks.

Soon after entering Loyola University law school in Chicago, Jack realized something startling about the legal profession. Very few, if any, attorneys were good at public speaking. He thought that odd because of the nature of the work. In fact, he learned that most attorneys never even face a jury in their entire careers, some never even going inside a courtroom, spending their years tied to oars in the belly of the boat, rowing away their lives in servitude to big law firms whose clients were corporations. Nobody who applies to law school aspires to such boring work, in fact they're surprised when they land their first job and it's heartbreakingly mundane, the higher-up lawyers insensitive, the partners aloof, the office politics cutthroat and mean.

He also found out after taking his first job that most lawyers are pricks, especially the ones from the Ivy League schools. They were as common in Boston as oysters on ice in the restaurants on the harbor. He relished the fact that he was a kid from Carthage, Illinois who lived by the seat of his pants, entertained juries and made tons of money doing it. It was even easier now that he had younger attorneys working for him who did his research, something he dreaded when he was working alone. The boring work of research, slaving away at law libraries well into the night, had never been his forte. Shoddy research was a killer before judges and prosecutors, but juries were different, they relied more on intuition, horse-sense to reach their decisions. Case law was largely irrelevant to them, judge's instructions a foreign language. Most jury members left the courtroom shaking their heads, surprised and shocked that this was American justice at work. It's like so many businesses, the more you learn about it the more you realize it's all screwed up, it just stumbles along and somehow it gets the job done. A good friend in the restaurant business told him that at the really fancy restaurants the food was always falling on the floor back in the kitchen and chefs would just pick it up with their hands and plop it back on the plate. Another buddy, a psychiatrist, told him that most diagnoses were just crude guesses, sometimes not even that good.

Lucky for him he now made gobs of money because he had two ex-wives to support plus a son at an overpriced liberal arts college in Maine, a whole lot different from the one he'd attended for the first two years, Spoon River Community College in Illinois, named after a real river that inspired Spoon River Anthology, the masterpiece by Edgar Lee Masters. The college in Maine was so insufferably smug that Jack hated to pour thousands of dollars each year into its coffers. He'd asked the president of the school where they recruited their students, the answer from the bow-tied chin-stroker "We don't recruit, they come to us." La-de-fucking-da. So many people in New England and Boston had their noses in the air, a big drawback to living there, Jack thought, so different from western Illinois where everybody was pretty plain and simple, what you saw is what you got.

Jack didn't get into law to make a lot of money. It just happened to work out that way. He didn't overworry about money, thinking that if everything stopped today he'd still be able to hang a shingle and eke out a living doing what he enjoyed. But the money sure made life easier, always does. Money may not necessarily make you happier, but it solves a shitload of irritating problems. For example, he always drove a nice car, and money was the reason he no longer needed a bungee cord to make sure his trunk closed. And he had the best shower nozzles in town. And on and on.

CHAPTER 3

CORNELIUS BONOMONO

I've known Jack for a long time and every once in a while we would get together for lunch, usually some out-of-the-way place that had a bar, too. Jack got me out of the first jam I was in with the law, and got me out of a few others as well. I never met anyone who was as good as him when it came to surfing the legal system. He was the kind of guy who comes off as not so special, maybe even a little dumb, and then wham he hits you with something that is really smart. That's how he was in court, and with other lawyers. It was a sight to see when he came up against other lawyers, them with all their nice clothes and perfect haircuts and in walks Jack, looking like the guy who might work down at some department store. Then he'd hit them with some legal mumbo jumbo that would floor them. He wasn't just my lawyer, he was also my friend. I can trust Jack and there aren't many people you can trust in this world.

When I was a kid we used to run around on the streets all day down on the South End of Boston, sometimes play basketball but most of the time just hang out and get in some trouble every once in a while, stealing from some of the stores. My mom worked and my dad...well, my dad we'd see him go in and out of buildings in the neighborhood. I only learned later that he was a bagman for one of the mafia guys downtown, and he was like their buttboy, doing all sorts of odd jobs for them. It used to make me feel bad that my dad was a gofer, but he was a good dad, and he kept us four kids in line and I know he loved my mom. Too bad he died so young, but he never took care of himself, chain-smoking and drinking. One day my mom found him in the easy chair in our front room at our apartment when she came home from work and he had probably been dead all day, his body cold. She collapsed on the floor and my aunt found her a half hour later and called the paramedics.

I was the chubby guy and I really liked sports but wasn't very good at it and I had to be the last guy they picked for teams but it didn't bother me too much because I liked to play all kinds of sports. You'd think with all the sports I would have lost weight but I figured that some people gotta be fat, and I was that guy. Nobody teased me much because I was strong too but I wasn't mean but they figured why mess with me, why not pick on another kid who's not so strong? I didn't do so well in school because I thought so many things seemed so much more interesting outside of school. I liked to watch what went on in the neighborhood, like the guy who ran a little fix-it shop and fixed all sorts of things for people. Sometimes I'd go in there just to see all the things he had lined up to fix and ask him about this thing or that thing. He got tired of me hanging out there so he told me to leave, but I kept going back and finally he just let me hang out as long as I didn't bother him. Eventually he came to like me and called me his "front-office guy" because I'd say hi to all of his customers.

There was a girl in the neighborhood who I liked but she never knew it. Like I said, I was the fat guy and I was sure she never even noticed me around and she probably liked guys like Ricky Moran who was built like a bodybuilder and had a big head of jet-black hair and was cool and kind of swung loose when he walked. He always seemed to have some money with him, too and I wondered where he got it because I knew his family was poor and that his dad was a drunk. He'd flash that cash in front of everybody and act like a bigshot.

 I found out where Ricky got his money, he was running errands for the Irish gangs in the neighborhood. Like the Italians the Irish pretty much took care of their own and Ricky wanted everybody to know that he was connected. When we were in high school I was still playing sports and one time we had a pick-up football game over at the park and I accidentally ran right into Ricky and flattened him to the ground. He started yelling at me and calling me a big fat shithead and left the game and walked away. I didn't mean to do it but I always felt that he held that against me, even when we got older and would see each other out and about. He always kind of sneered at me.

When I got a little older I started to lose some of my weight, and I started working out with the weights so I got even stronger. My dad and mom couldn't afford to even let me consider college, not even the community college over in Dorchester, so I started working at a warehouse over in Chelsea that dealt in auto parts for the whole Boston area. I worked with a bunch of great guys, almost all of us either Italians or Irish, and we worked our assess off and then sometimes got together at night and drank and hung around the bars. We were always telling each other bullshit stories about this girl or that girl and our sexual exploits but I knew nobody was getting anything. I wasn't.

Jimmy Cochran was one of the guys I worked with and he asked me one time if I wanted to make a little extra money helping his brother out on some jobs. I figured it was something his brother was doing on the side, maybe hauling furniture or something, so I said yeah, I'd like to make some more money. Who wouldn't?

It turns out that Jimmy and a few other guys had this deal where they would steal stuff from warehouses around town, and give the stuff to these other guys who did God knows what with this stuff. All I did was drive this truck, and wait until they loaded it up and then I'd drive it to this spot near the airport and somebody would unload it. For that I'd get almost $100 a night, and that was great because I was just adding it to the money I made at the auto parts warehouse. I was socking that money away in the bank.

I knew what I was doing, a lot of the guys in the neighborhood did this sort of stuff on the side to make ends meet, some even used the money to help send their kids to college, or make sure their daughter had a good wedding or to help out a relative who may have fallen onto hard times. I even knew one knucklehead who gave the extra money to the church! Back in our neighborhood people took care of each other, especially family. Family trumped everything.

They started asking me to do some other things besides just driving the truck, and said they needed a big guy with muscle to help them make sure people paid them on time the money they owed. I knew it was a loan shark business but they told me that they never really ever had to get rough with anyone, that just having a big guy in the background was enough to make sure people paid on time. It's not like it is on television or the movies, hardly ever was there any rough stuff and I never had to beat anybody up. Thank God it never came up because I don't think I could have done it. There were a lot of guys who had no problem doing those sorts of things but I wasn't one of them.

That's pretty much how it worked out, I was the muscle but I didn't have to use any of it, and I got paid pretty good money for just being around. I hooked up with Larry Olivetti and we got an apartment over near the airport and I moved out of my mom's house. It was a pretty fun time, hanging out in the neighborhood and working my regular job at the warehouse and picking up some good money at night working with both the Irish and Italian guys. Nothing we did was really very bad, mostly just stealing and doing the loan shark stuff. Larry he was a little more serious about the whole thing and was always pushing to do bigger stuff, but I was pretty happy doing what I was doing. Although I was as ambitious as the next guy, I never wanted to screw anyone to get ahead.

I got arrested one time on one of the nighttime jobs and I knew enough to say nothing to the cops. Don't open your yap except to give them your name. I asked Jack who lived next door to us if he could help me out. I could never figure why he lived in Chelsea when he worked downtown at some fancy law firm. He was from somewhere in the Midwest and he was a nice guy and we used to drink beer together on the back porch and shoot the shit. I told some of the Irish and Italian guys about Jack and they said maybe he was someone to go to if they got in trouble, too. When Larry got charged for beating that guy up he hired Jack and Jack got him out of that mess. Jack was really a very good lawyer. That downtown firm who fired him had no idea how good he was.

Life is funny because that girl I really liked in school turned out to like me too, and we started seeing each other. She was half Italian, half Irish, which is a great combination because they usually turn out to be very pretty people. With my job and my nighttime work and my girlfriend, life was just great for me, I couldn't have been happier. I ended up marrying her, Mary was her name, and she and I settled down in a small apartment at first in the Irish part of town. Her family was very accepting of me, which I worried about for a long time with me being Italian and kind of connected in a way, but at a very low level. The Irish and the Italians run most of Boston, but they are very different kinds of people, they keep their distance from one another but both know to get along you got to go along. There's a lot of things that separate them, but one of the things that really they had in common, at least in those days, was everybody was Catholic. The big St.

Joseph Days in the North End and the St. Patrick's Day parade downtown were the biggest celebrations every year and everybody went to both, Irish and Italian.

Wouldn't you know that Mary got pregnant right off the bat, we figured probably just a week after we got married, and she was upset a lot at first because she didn't want to have kids so fast, she wanted some years where it was just her and me. At the time she was working downtown in a woman's clothing store and with the money we both made life was pretty good, there was spending money for stuff we'd never had before. Mary is the kind of girl who is always up, happy, and cuts me lots of slack. She's gorgeous, too, and my friends always said it was amazing that a big ugly guy like me snagged such a beauty.

My work was getting busy and all of a sudden I was in demand by a lot of different groups because of my size and because I looked like some tough guy from a Hollywood movie about mobsters. In fact once Mary told me maybe I should try out for a part in a movie since I looked the part. She didn't know about some of the work I did and thought all of the money came from my regular job, with me telling her I was getting bonuses for this and that, which in a way was what I was doing. I never told Mary very much about my extracurricular work, although she is smart and had to know that all the money we had wasn't just coming from a job at an auto parts warehouse. But she never pried into my business very much, and I never pried into her business either.

When our son arrived I was probably the happiest man in the world. Me, Mary and Tony were a constant threesome and every Saturday or Sunday if I wasn't working we'd go down to the harbor for a walk and just look at the sights downtown. Mary quit her job as soon as Tony came along and with my salary and the money from the extra jobs we were able to make it pretty good. I always thanked God that I made enough money for Mary to stay home with Tony because I never liked it when mothers left their tiny kids in daycare. Kids need a mother around, that's what I believe. Old school that way. I'm old school in most ways, and I don't necessarily give a damn what other people think.

CHAPTER 4

JACK LAPOINT

When the police came to my office looking for Larry Olivetti I lied to them about where he was and just told them I didn't know. But I knew where he was, in an apartment attached to a warehouse. I knew enough to know why they were looking for him. It didn't have anything to do with me or my law practice, and I didn't have anything to do with the guy either legally or otherwise. Where Cornelius had kept pretty much to the straight and narrow in the crime world, doing smalltime stuff, Olivetti had crossed over into the more serious business of doing the dirty work for the big gangs in Boston. I always thought Olivetti had a really violent side, probably was a psychopath, and Cornelius was a buffer between the two of us back then. But I never liked being alone with Olivetti, always wanted Cornelius to be there with us. When I moved out of Chelsea that was the last I saw of Olivetti, and I thought good riddance. I was hoping that the cops would find Olivetti and put him away somewhere for years and get him off the streets. But I wasn't going to tell them anything, never wanted to come anywhere near getting mixed up with that guy.

This was just a few months before I had a partner and I was still working alone, making more money than ever before. The drug dealers knew to come to me, and the guys who stole stuff, and the guys who beat up other people trying to collect for the loan sharks. Other lawyers knew I was a bottom-feeder, but the way I figured it I was my own boss, not slaving away for some rich-ass partners downtown, putting in my time before they even offered me some shitty proposition to be a junior partner when I'm 45 years old.

There's something about being your own boss that is so invigorating, so righteous. I used to occasionally bump into some of the lawyers at the old firm where I was fired from and they'd tell me about all the office politics and the endless meetings and the prick attorneys they had to work with, and I'd think to myself what a wonderful thing it is to work for yourself. The only bad thing is you have to get all your own business, and you have to do everything from typing up your own letters to doing your own copying on the Xerox machine. My name was on the firm's front door and it was on there twice just to make sure.

My firm was starting to take off in a big way and I had to buy time from some attorneys I knew downtown to handle some of the extra cases that came my way. There was a gal I knew, Shelly, who came in from time to time and we got to like each other. She worked at the cab company down the street where I used to go to have all my photocopies done. I didn't go there anymore because I could afford my own copying machines by then, but I had met Shelly down there from before. We did stuff together, she was five years younger than me, and she wanted to be a nurse. I wouldn't say she was a beauty, but I loved her sense of humor and the fact that she never backed down from anybody, kind of fearsome like I'd never seen in a woman before, except maybe my own mother. Other than that she was nothing like my mom. I saw her face down a big galoot down at the taxi cab company who came in raging mad about something, and she did it without flinching or batting an eye.

She loved sex even more than I did, and that was saying a lot. Sometimes we'd stay in bed all day on Saturdays, leaving at night to eat a big dinner on the North End. She also liked to do drugs, but I stayed away from that part of it. After all, I had a business to run and I couldn't afford to be fucked up. She loved the cocaine and said it made the sex feel even better. I thought it felt damn good without any drugs.

Shelly didn't listen to me when I told her she can't be a nurse if she's using drugs, that they don't want drug users having instant access to drugs in the hospitals. I knew a guy who was in Alcoholics Anonymous and asked him what I might suggest to Shelly about coming clean. He told me that it's impossible to talk someone into coming clean, they have to come to that conclusion all on their own. But he said he'd talk with her if I wanted him to, just to bring it up. Maybe he'd invite her to one of their meetings and if she liked it maybe she could come to another meeting.

The long and the short of it was this guy and Shelly started seeing each other, although I didn't know it for a couple of months. She just wasn't around much for a while, and I thought maybe she was coming clean, struggling with her problem and doing something about it. Come to find out that I'm on the North End one night walking with a couple of friends and who comes down the street together but this guy and Shelly, walking hand in hand. I can't remember ever losing my temper even when I was a kid but then and there I started screaming at the two of them, going for this guy like I was a hockey player on the sideboards. My buddies dragged me off the guy, and I stood back and screamed at Shelly about how could she stab me in the back like that? My friends took me back to their car and drove me home, me in the back seat almost curled up like a kid. I was so hurt, really.

Funny thing was this other guy was able to get Shelly clean, and they got married a year later, and made big successes of their lives. I'd see them around Boston from time to time after that, this guy becoming sort of a tycoon in a downtown brokerage, and Shelly did go to nursing school and worked down at Brigham and Women's. I never did get over their treachery and harbored a grudge against both of them for years, which is sort of unlike me to do that. I usually forget about shit after a few months, which is a blessing. I didn't say I have a forgiving nature, but a forgetting nature. When somebody does me wrong in a year's time someone else has to remind me that it even happened. I think that's a good thing, because you don't remember any grudges. The Irish and the Italians, they hold grudges, and have very long memories. Me, I forget a lot of things.

I met Barbara soon after that, she was a friend of one of my buddies, a guy by the name of McIntosh who's a real Irish character. He's the guy who hooked us up, ambushed me really by not telling me he was inviting her to one of our outings down on the cape when we used to rent a cottage every summer near Hyannis. She and I hit it off right away, and when I came home I called her right up and we started seeing each other. She was everything I wanted in a woman, she was funny, made me laugh, and had a body that turned me on no end. I was at that age where I figured it was time to settle down and have kids and get a regular house in the suburbs. My firm was growing, and I thought it was the time to make that sort of big leap in life. Many of my friends were settling down, even the guys I thought would never. So, I joined the crowd.

She was from a good family, too, over in Brookline, and her parents were the kind of people who were proper Boston people, formal in a way that only Boston people can be. I remember the first time she had the four of us meet, in a fancy downtown restaurant on a snowy Saturday night. Her parents were the kind of WASPish people I'd see all over Boston, even though they were Catholic. I could tell that her mom was kind of cold, but the dad wanted to be livelier but kept looking at his wife to see how he should act. They asked me where I was from and I told them all about Carthage and Hancock County and that my dad had been an attorney, and that I started out in Chicago, got hired to go to Boston, and started my own firm. I was still working out of the office in Chelsea and when they heard that their faces fell, even though they tried to hide it. There's no way to dress up the fact that Chelsea is anything but where the lowlifes lived. Barbara was getting nervous, hoping this wasn't a deal breaker for them. But I recouped when I said that I'd be taking on a partner soon, and moving downtown. I liked the dad much more than the mother. At the end of the night I'd passed the test with a C-plus or maybe even a B. Barbara said I did better than that, but she said the big thing they didn't like is I wasn't Catholic.

You know my life in many ways is like that of Edgar Lee Masters, who once was a really popular writer during the 1930s and 1940s but most people don't know about now. I love his stuff and think he's one of the titans of American literature. He had also grown up in a small town in Illinois and was the son of a guy who struggled financially with a failing law practice, just as my dad had. Masters eventually started a very successful law practice in Chicago and for eight years his partner was the famous defense attorney Clarence Darrow. Masters though was more a poet and writer than a lawyer and his masterpiece, Spoon River Anthology, is actually a long poem, a collection of monologues from the dead people in an Illinois cemetery. How about that for a subject for a book? It is haunting in its commentary about small town life, really about life everywhere. The town portrayed in the book is a combination of Lewistown, where Masters grew up, and Petersburg, where my grandparents had lived. I know both towns very well and the book is so much like what I recalled about my own home town that it raises chills up my spine whenever I re-read it, which is about every two years. I really wish I had known the guy, would love to have had an evening with him, ask him questions about the law and where in the hell did he ever come up with the idea for such a masterpiece as Spoon River Anthology. I'd also ask him what was Clarence Darrow like?

My hometown of Carthage actually has one big claim to fame or I guess you could say, infamy. It was where Joseph Smith, the founder of the Mormons, was murdered. Smith had been jailed in Carthage on charges of ordering the destruction of the Nauvoo Expositor, a newspaper whose first and only edition revealed he was practicing polygamy. Smith and his brother Hyrum voluntarily surrendered to the authorities to face the charges against them and while they were in jail awaiting trial an armed mob of men with painted faces stormed the jail and shot and killed both men. In those days of the frontier the concept of due process was not yet fully understood or appreciated. Another thing back then is trials were very short, and punishments meted out the next day, or as soon as they could build a scaffold. Wouldn't be a bad thing to bring that back for some cases today.

Home is where you grow up, not where you currently live. When someone mentioned "home" to me it immediately conjured in my mind western Illinois where I was raised. Although New England is gorgeous, especially in the fall, it's the pancake-flat land of Hancock County that's home, although I haven't been there for a long time. I own a beautiful summer house on Lake Sunapee in New Hampshire and love the time I spend there, but it's the Mississippi that I really love. But that's long ago and far away and my ex-wives and even my son look down their noses at what they think is the unsophisticated Midwest, maybe grudgingly giving Chicago some points for having a couple of universities and a few skyscrapers. There are a few other people in Boston who come from western Illinois or Northeast Missouri and when we run into one another we huddle together and share stories about what we miss about home. What do we all miss the most? Answer: the people are friendlier.

Too bad that part of the country isn't any place to make a living. The money is in New York, Boston, Chicago, San Francisco. In fact, I haven't been back to Carthage in nearly ten years when my mother died. My sister and brother left Carthage years ago, too, and they haven't been back either. My brother is one of those IT wizards in Silicon Valley and makes a ton of money and my sister lives in Omaha with six grown children, and she has a ton of money too because her husband was one of the early investors with Warren Buffet's Berkshire Hathaway outfit. I guess you could say that we all made good. I'm glad my mother lived long enough to see us grow up into successes. We make sure to get together once a year, usually in San Francisco. When we're together we tell the same old stories about my mom and dad and growing up in that house in Carthage, and sometimes the stories are so funny that we end up laughing till we cry. I'd have to say that the family I grew up in was a happy bunch.

I live by myself in the Back Bay near Boston University in a beautiful two-story condominium overlooking the Charles River where I can see the college rowing teams going through their paces, cutting perfect wakes in precision timing. The Charles is about as different from the Mississippi as you could imagine. If they were brothers the Charles would be the slender, sophisticated one, the Mississippi smelly and wild and powerful. The Charles is neutered, the Mississippi has balls. The closest I can come to a semi-wild river is the Connecticut River about twenty miles west of my lake house, and that's only about a quarter of the size of the Mississippi.

In the way of all remembrances my view of Carthage, Hancock County and the Mississippi are heavily tinted with good memories reassembled in my mind to fit my own needs. If I were to return to live there it would be colorless, boring. But lately I think more about my childhood and adolescence there maybe because I'm getting older and an older guy starts to try and make some sense out of his life, how everything fits together. It was the place where I was young, strong, carefree, bursting with energy and ambition, every day an adventure. Maybe that weird feeling I get in the morning about something hanging over my head is the realization that my life is finite and that I'm much closer to my end than to my beginning. There's an old saying in the Bible that most people are given "three score and ten" – 70 years, and it hasn't changed all that much in all those years, except many live maybe 15 years longer, but a lot of them have to live in those awful nursing homes to do it. I wish I had a dollar for everyone who's told me they'd rather die than go to a nursing home. Obviously they're lying because the nursing homes are packed with people. Maybe you change your mind as you reach old age, and you say to yourself okay maybe a couple of years more before I meet my maker.

My partners Larry Maguire and Leland Stockwell are very different from me, thank God. Larry joined me shortly after I'd moved my office out of Chelsea and I first met him downtown where he was working for one of the big firms like I had been doing when I first got to Boston. He was Boston all the way, even went to Boston College and then Boston University for law school. He is Catholic through and through. When I was growing up it seemed I didn't know any Catholics and in Boston it seemed that I didn't know anyone who wasn't Catholic, although many of them weren't practicing. I found out, though, that "not practicing" doesn't mean they're not Catholic. One of my buddies, also Catholic, naturally, told me that being Catholic was with you no matter what religion you said you were later, even if you said you were an atheist. I've also found out that if a lapsed Catholic is really sick they mostly scramble back to the church, probably figuring they'll hedge their bets.

Larry and I get along really well although his wife Sheila thinks I'm an asshole. I think she's a stuck-up WASP. Leland Stockwell joined us a couple of years later, and he's a quiet kind of guy and a genius at finding technicalities that often result in either dropped prosecutions or not guilty verdicts. Both of them are very good at what they do, and it's a blessing we all get along well both in and out of the office. We make a great team, and the success of the firm shows it.

Just because I'm the founder of the firm doesn't mean I can just lay back and collect my checks. I still have to hustle for new business, work my ass off on big cases and ride herd on the junior attorneys. When it comes to management I'm always the soft touch, Leland and Larry more hard-assed with the attorneys. I just find it hard to come down hard on them, especially the young attorneys because when I look at them I think of myself when I was that age and how much I hated some of the prick attorneys I had to work with. Why do so many pricks rise so high in the world?

We meet every week with all the other attorneys to plan out our upcoming litigation. They always want to push me in front of the juries because I have a reputation for being a good speaker, and humorous when I need to be, serious when that's needed. I don't want to brag, but what juries like about me is I'm just a regular guy going about my work, and that's really me. I buy my suits at Men's Warehouse and I wear shoes I buy at Penneys. I even cut my own hair and my second wife always said it looked like shit. I think I do a good job on my hair and I never understood why some guys pay fifty bucks for a haircut. I'm not a skinflint, I'll spend money on some things, like the lake house. But mostly I'm pretty modest in my purchases, and have a tendency to save money. Always good to have something stashed away for a rainy day.

If I have one big fault it's women. I love them. I love their company and it's not just about sex. I'm equally comfortable around men, but they have to be of a certain type. They got to be cynical, funny, not the rah-rah types. I don't like being around optimists. My love of women is maybe why I got two ex-wives. But I wasn't fooling around on them, they were fooling around on me. I'm still friendly with them, Barbara my first wife and the mother of our son, and Jocelyn, my second wife. They both met men they liked better than me. With Barbara it hurt like hell, but with Jocelyn I wasn't so happy with her, either, so it was a very amicable split, although I couldn't stand the ass-wipe she had for a divorce attorney. If Barbara came to me today and said she wanted to get back with me I'd do it in a second, but I don't think that's going to happen. I see her around town from time to time and she's with this guy she left me for, and she looks really happy and even though we get along, it pains me to see her looking so happy with this guy. I think the guy is okay, but the few times I talked with him I couldn't look him in the eye without thinking hey this guy is sleeping with my wife!

Our son, William, isn't like me. He's a scholarly type with a touch of elitism about him and he wants to be a college professor and researcher. I love him dearly and would do anything for him but I realize that he identifies more with his mother than he does to me. I try my best with him and he knows I love him but we never can get into a natural rhythm beyond superficial conversations. He comes up to the lake house from time to time and we go out on the boat and do some fishing, but there's moments of silence between us that I know makes him feel awkward, and make me feel awkward, too. Oh well, you can't have everything. I love him to death. I think he knows that, at least I hope so.

I never quite figured out why my two marriages ended and why they both found other guys they loved and liked better than me. I thought I was a good husband but maybe I worked too hard and didn't pay as much attention to them as I should have. I never played around on either of them, and provided them a really good lifestyle. The fact that we're all still friends, or at least talking from time to time, shows that I'm not a guy to hold any grudges, so it wasn't as if I was a prick to be around. Maybe sometimes it's just bad luck, or the fact that sometimes you can't control who you're going to meet down the road who you fall in love with, regardless of whether you're married or not. I think that's what happened to both of my wives. I've been around a lot of guys and women who have fallen in love with someone else other than their spouses, and I always think it's because they got married too young and never played the field, got a taste of being in a serious relationship with someone else before they got married.

CHAPTER 5

WALTER STRAW

The case that skyrocketed Jack's firm to the really big time in Boston was what Jack called the "Clash of the Titans." One of the city's wealthiest and most established finance guys – Walter Straw -- had allegedly raped a woman from an equally wealthy family from one of Boston's oldest blue-blood families, Ruth Silverton. The rape had allegedly occurred at a pre-Christmas party at the woman's home in Wellesley, in the upstairs bedroom used by her young son, who was gone for the weekend. Later that night, after the party, she called the police and claimed she'd been raped by Straw. A rape kit examination showed she'd had intercourse, and a semen sample was taken. Straw was arrested and arraigned and the media had a field day.

Straw's brother Joseph had called Jack and asked him to speak with Walter, who had easily made bail. The meeting took place downtown in an office near the Boston Common. Jack was shown into a plush boardroom, offered coffee and refreshments, and waited five minutes until the two brothers entered the room. Introductions were made. Everything was very formal yet subdued. Really rich people rarely get very excited, never need to, Jack figured, they feel bulletproof.

"Mr. LaPoint, please understand that you are on retainer at this point but we've not officially retained you as counsel for the case, but consider this meeting highly confidential," Joseph said. He was obviously the older brother, used to being in charge, although his manner was soft, confident. Jack had heard that Joseph would try to take charge, he was the brains of the family, and not unfamiliar with errant behavior himself, although most of it was back in his youth.

"Walter, please tell Mr. LaPoint what you told me," Joseph said, looking at his younger brother, who sat at the table like a high school student waiting outside the vice principal's office. Walter looked down at his lap, bit his lip, and then raised his head and looked at Jack.

"Well, we did have sex, I'll say that right from the start. There's no denying that. But she was the one who initiated it, she came on to me earlier in the evening.

We went up to the bedroom and one thing led to another and that was it. We went back down to the party," Walter said, looking Jack directly in the eye. Good sign, Jack thought. First impressions mean a lot, and Jack didn't see any telltale signs yet that the guy was lying.

"We're either or both of your drinking?" Jack asked. It usually figured in a lot of sexual assault cases.

"Yes."

"How much?"

"Me, I was what I'd call at the happy stage of drinking. Two martinis, at about the top before you get a little sick," he said. Good way to put it, Jack thought, believable.

"What about her?"

"I'd say she was about the same stage, maybe even a little more on the sloppy side."

"Give me the details," Jack said.

"Well, we were obviously interested in one another. She came on to me, even kind of nuzzling herself next to me....," Walter started.

"Sorry for interrupting, but did anyone witness this?" Jack asked.

"Somebody must have noticed it, it was pretty obvious to me, but we were in one of the side rooms, off from the main room where most of the people were," Walter said.

Walter went on to explain that Ruth Silverton offered to take Walter on a tour of the house, and the two went upstairs. After looking at several of the rooms, maybe in the space of five minutes, they ended up in what she said was her son's room. "She was the first one to touch me, you know that kind of touch on your chest where it indicates a woman is interested in getting physical?" Walter asked.

Jack didn't nod his head in agreement. He was asking the questions.

"Then we sat down on the bed and started kissing. Then she was the one to start massaging me in the crotch. I got up and closed the door. I didn't want anybody seeing us. I took her shirt off, down to her bra. She helped me out of my pants but my shirt was still on. She started playing with my penis, and I took her bra off, and then it just went from there."

"Did anyone ever come upstairs, open the door or anything?"

"No."

Joseph interrupted. "I think this looks like a clear case of consensual sex."

Jack didn't say anything in response, but watched the two brothers look at one another. As always, Jack followed his number one rule, nothing is ever as it seems. Nothing is clear-cut. His sense was that Walter was telling the truth. But he wasn't going to lecture Joseph, not at this introductory meeting. Joseph seemed like the guy who would feel that any challenge to his authority was an assault on the family honor. Challenging Joseph would be unproductive at this early stage. Besides, he wanted to become the attorney of record in this case, it would boost his firm into the stratosphere in Boston legal circles.

"What do you think?" Joseph asked Jack.

"Well….forgive me for being blunt, but she went to the police shortly after that and said she was raped. That's on her side of the ledger in this case. But, on the opposite side of the ledger there may be people at the party who could testify that they saw her coming on to Walter, 'nuzzling' as you said. That's hard to ignore at a party."

"I'd say those two things cancel each other out, so we're left with a he said/she said situation, but there's been a charge filed. The answer to that is in gathering up enough on our side to make it seem reasonable to a jury or a judge that this was consensual."

Jack explained it would involve taking an exhaustive look into the woman's background – had she had affairs before, had she come on to other men, had she had counseling for such things as sex addiction, was she mentally ill?

"Please think carefully back to that evening, and if you recall anything that might help your case, let me know," Jack said. "And, if you recall anything that may hurt your case, do the same, let me know."

"Oh, by the way, they're going to do the same with you. They'll examine your history as well, so if there's anything there we need to know about, get it out now," Jack advised.

Here was the important point in a conversation with a client charged in a crime. A person's reaction at this point is to manage to forget an important piece in their history that may turn out to be devastating if it becomes known later in a trial. Jack thought he'd go for it.

"You ever been charged in any sex-related cases?" he asked Walter.

Walter and Joseph looked at one another. That didn't bode well.

"Well…there was something that happened in college. A woman said that I raped her," Walter said, sheepishly.

Now all bets were off.

"Tell me about that," Jack said.

"Well, I was a sophomore, we were in a fraternity house at a party, and she said I raped her. We were both drunk. She didn't go to the police until a week later, and then it was the college police. It went through the college system, but I was finally exonerated, they couldn't come up with any evidence that anything had happened. "

"Did you rape her, Walter?"

"No, it was the same as this one. She came on to me, we were drunk."

Jack again sensed Walter was telling the truth. Despite that the record of the college incident would be used like a cudgel against Walter in this case. He'd have to figure out a way to mitigate this in some way before this went to trial. Best way to handle it was bring it up first, get it out in the open, and explain it away. Or get it excluded by the court.

"Anything else you want to tell me. Be frank," Jack said.

"Nothing," Walter answered.

No case was ever easy, nothing ever a slam dunk, no matter what the initial findings were. Stories wound around like snakes in a basket, and you could get bit at any time. Despite what Jack thought about Walter the man could be lying his ass off. Or maybe it was Joseph who'd had an affair with Ruth, and Ruth was just trying to get back at him by fucking his brother. The only facts on the table were that Walter and Ruth had sex, he'd inserted his penis into her vagina and ejaculated and that a couple of hours later she called the police to report a rape. There was a sample of semen taken. Everything else was up for grabs.

Regardless, the case was front-page material, cat-nip for the media. A win for Jack LaPoint was as good as gold.

The case went to trial, a no-holds-barred slugfest that sucked in some of Boston's top names. Even the people who had attended the party lawyered up. Experts were brought in by the busload, private detectives and computer hackers were used by both sides to dig out every morsel of background on both parties involved. Jury selection alone took a week, each side jockeying to make sure there was the proper number of each gender on the panel.

Like so many trials it boiled down to a trust contest between Silverton and Walter Straw. Jack was able to deftly explain away the college assault charge, making it seem that the woman then had victimized Walter, not the other way around. Silverton had just enough of a tainted history with men to make her story sound suspicious. Besides, there were two witnesses who testified that they had seen Silverton brush her leg up against Straw. That was probably the deciding factor. The jury deliberated for about nine hours before delivering a verdict – not guilty.

After the verdict was read Walter turned to Jack and shook his hand.

"Thank you," he said in a quiet voice.

Then, Walter turned, embracing his brother Joseph. Jack overheard Joseph tell his brother "We really dodged the bullet this time."

This time?

Jack didn't know which way to interpret that remark. Would it not have been better at that emotional moment to have said "Thank God?"

Jack put his papers in his briefcase, people were coming up to him patting him on the back, shaking his hand. He looked briefly over at the prosecutor's table, the two attorneys were packing up their briefcases. Ruth Silverton was hunched over, sobbing.

Such is the law, Jack thought.

This time? The two words confounded him.

The end chapter in the sordid story of Walter and Ruth could not have been dreamed up by even the best suspense writer. Less than a month after the verdict Ruth approached Walter in the lobby of the Union League Club, walked right up to him, spit in his face, and pulled a small revolver from her handbag. She shot him through the left eye, screamed out "bastard" and dropped the gun on the tile floor. She stood over the body and kicked the corpse until someone came up from behind and pulled her away.

"This time?" Jack thought when he was told the news. Well, he didn't dodge the bullet this time. He wondered who would defend Ruth Silverton.

CHAPTER 6

RUTH SILVERTON

It was like one of those dreams where you want to run away from something bad and your legs won't work. That's what it was like from the time I called the cops to say I'd been raped to the second I heard the not guilty verdict. I was raped and it was like I couldn't get one damn person to take me seriously. That attorney LaPoint I grew to loathe and he turned everything around so much that I was the one guilty and not Walter Straw, who pinned me to my son's bed and pumped semen deep inside me. Straw had me down on the bed so fast that my brain couldn't keep up with what was going on and I know I kept saying no, no, no from the very beginning. I was a little bit drunk but not so drunk that I didn't know what was going on. When I walked downstairs after I was raped there were still a few guests there but I don't really remember speaking with anyone, I was in a state of shock, almost catatonic. I sat down in a back room and tried to organize my mind. After about an hour and a half I called 911.

I learned that in court they can make you look any way they need you to look, they can dredge something up about you from 20 years ago that was innocent but make it sound so bad. They can find old enemies, even old friends, who say uncomplimentary things about you and make you sound evil. That's what they did to me. They had me coming on to Walter like a panther in heat and they turned an inadvertent brush-up against him into a full blown seduction. I was a little drunk and I swayed into him, and that was it. Two people saw it and that lawyer made it sound like I bared my breasts to him. It was even Walter's suggestion that I give him a tour of the upstairs and I almost had a stroke when I heard him say what happened upstairs. It was a lie from beginning to end. He made himself look so victimized by me and the jury bought the whole damn lie. To that jury I was the vixen who led this guy all along and then claimed it was rape. It was rape!

When I got home that night after the verdict I went right up to my bedroom and just sat in the dark all night, I don't think I moved a muscle. I watched the sun come up and decided that my life was over, that forever I'd be the seducer who destroyed that nice man, the woman who willingly offered herself up and spread her legs and then screamed rape.

CHAPTER 7

LARRY MAGUIRE

You would have thought I'd have been smarter. When I joined up with Jack LaPoint we were just two guys on the make, taking on the world. It was a lot of fun back then because the stakes were still fairly low and the clients were loosey-goosey, things seemed clearer, cleaner then. Once we got all fancy things got a lot more complicated and fuzzy. I was always the guy trying to one-up everybody, trying to score just a bit more money, a little more status, pats on the back from friends. I liked to intimidate those guys I didn't like. I thought I was one hot shit back then.

Jack was my age but I always thought of him as my mentor, I looked up to the guy. He's not fancy like a lot of the other people in the legal scene in Boston, but pretty down home and I like the fact that he came from some nowhere place in Illinois and made a big name for himself in Boston where most people think it's the center of the entire universe and no civilization exists elsewhere. When I started going out with Sheila she didn't like him from the get-go and I can't explain why. He didn't say much to her that first time we all got together, in fact he didn't talk much as I recall. But Sheila told me that night that she didn't think he was very smart, kind of a hick and unsophisticated. I told her that was exactly part of Jack's appeal, that he actually was whip-smart but hid it under this act that he was just a bumpkin sometimes. I just thought that Sheila would get to like Jack more once she got to know him, but it never happened that way, I just had to make sure that she didn't have to be around him much. It's funny how some people just take a disliking to someone and it stays that way no matter what the other person does. As a result I don't think Jack took much a shine to Sheila either.

Jack and I started making tons of money and that's something I just loved. When the checks would come in and some of them were five figures I'd be overjoyed. I'd even wait for the mail to come in the office and open those checks right away and look them over, handle them. Jack was happy to have the money, too, but he didn't seem to get as excited as me about it. My family never had much at all and it was exhilarating to be making so much and I was still pretty young. My mom and dad were so pleased with what I'd made of myself and I treated them to all sorts of things, even paid off their mortgage and bought them a new car. Life was very good. But it seemed like the money came in one door and went out the other.

Being too excited about money was probably why it all started, how I got myself into this situation I am in now. I'd been working with Jack for about a dozen years already and one night when I was drinking down in the North End I got into a conversation with this guy next to me at the bar. He was big and burly and seemed like a nice guy and it turns out that he worked for Sonny Ianetta, the big crime boss in Boston, although I didn't know it at the time and he didn't say that. When he found out what my job was we exchanged phone numbers and he said let's keep in touch, he may be in need of my services someday. That was the end of the conversation. That stuff happened all the time, you meet somebody and exchange phone numbers.

It didn't even seem important at the time and I kind of forgot it but about a year later I got a call from this guy and he had to remind me of our conversation in the bar. His name was Jimmy Tracadora and if I could rewind time I would have never gone into that bar where I met him in the first place. But I later realized that I was so greedy if it hadn't been that meeting that got me in trouble it would have been just another down the road.

He wanted me to come meet his boss Sonny Ianetta and I went to a place in the North End that looked like the back room of a restaurant. My mistake was I didn't tell Jack about any of this, and maybe at that point Jack would have warned me about this stuff. Jack represented a lot of bad people, but he always told me to stay away from the big crime bosses, they were bad news and once you get hooked up with them they own you lock, stock and barrel. I had known of Sonny Ianetta because it was well known he was the crime boss on the North End. I thought what the hell, what harm is there in meeting with the guy? I should have never gone to that meeting. But again, the way I was going in those days, all cocky and sure of myself, it was inevitable that eventually I'd fall into the tiger pit.

Well, the meeting was all nicey-nice and I thought these guys aren't like the mob guys in the movies. They're not like what you see in The Godfather. They just seemed like regular guys. After we talked for about ten minutes they told me to think about something. These guys didn't even want me to work for them officially. They just wanted me to be their part-time legal consultant, that's what they called it. No one would have to know I worked for them, I wouldn't have to go to court or anything, all I had to do was be the back-stop lawyer who double-checked the work they were getting from other lawyers they had working for them. There'd be no paperwork, nothing. The other lawyers wouldn't even know I was in the picture. They made it sound like they wanted me to run down to the dry cleaners for them, they made it sound so simple.

I thought what they were describing sounded a little strange, but then they told me they would pay me a fee, and it was a whopper -- $10,000 a month to begin with, and all I had to do would take up maybe a handful of hours a month and that I'd be paid every month in cash so I didn't have to pay any tax on it. I couldn't believe what I was hearing, but I acted like people came up to me every day with deals like that, tried to act blasé.

I wouldn't normally go for something that sounded too good to be true, but they put that in front of me at just the right time. Even though I was making tons of money at the firm I was deep in debt. Tuition bills were piling up for the private schools for our daughters, and the big house we just bought in Wellesley, and the country club, and Sheila was one hell of a spending machine all on her own, never mind me, who was no slouch in that department. I'd lent money to two of my brothers and they couldn't pay me back and I had even bought a house for my parents, a gift to them. As I said the money came in one door and out the other. But eventually not enough was coming in the front, but a lot was going out.

They always say don't make a deal with the devil but that's exactly what I did. It didn't seem like that for a couple of years, and I never told Jack about my work for them on the side. I hardly ever even saw Sonny or his guys, and most of the time I could do the work at home. Maybe I wasn't keeping records but they were, and they made sure that I was on a leash. They upped the ante on me after a couple of years and asked me to do a couple of things that I shouldn't be doing. I did not realize it but the more stuff I knew about their business – and I was getting to know a lot – was a ball and chain on me. I came to realize that these guys would kill me in the blink of an eye if they thought me disloyal. I was part of the mob and being part of the mob doesn't include the option of going to the boss one day and saying you're giving your two-week notice and seeking other opportunities. It doesn't work that way. Once you've entered the organization there is only one way out, and everybody knew what that was. They had me by the balls and they knew it and I knew it. I wasn't very blasé anymore about all of this.

CHAPTER 8

THE FIRST KILLING

Jack's secretary poked her head into Jack's office. "You got a call. She says her name is Lucy Wetterau. She says she knows you?"

"Who?"

"She says her name is Lucy Wetterau. From Carthage"

For a moment Jack didn't recognize the name, it then came to him.

"Oh, Lucy Wetterau! It used to be Tozzini. Lucy Tozzini!"

"You want to take it?"

He momentarily hesitated, a bit flummoxed.

"Sure, send it along."

Lucy. He hadn't spoken with her in years. My God, why would she be calling?

The phone buzzer activated. He pressed the button.

"Lucy?"

"Jack...Jack, it's me, Lucy. Remember me?"

"Remember you, how could I forget you? It's been such a long time, Lucy," he said, not knowing what else to say. "How are you?"

"Jack, Jack...I'm in a bad fix and I couldn't think of anybody else to call. I need a lawyer."

"What happened?"

"They said I killed a guy. I didn't do it, but they've got me under arrest. I need a lawyer and I don't know any except you."

"Lucy, it's been what...twenty-five years? This is kind of a bolt out of the blue."

Lucy spoke fast, breathlessly. "Slow down, Lucy," he told her.

"Okay, okay. There's this guy I know, his name is...was...Eddie Crane. I met him over in Hamilton. He must have got in some trouble with some bad guys and they killed him. But the way it looks to the police is that I did it. But you know, Jack, I wouldn't hurt a flea, you know me. Eddie had his throat cut, there was blood all over. Oh, please Jack help me, I'm so afraid."

"Calm down Lucy, calm down. Where are you?"

"I'm in jail. In Carthage."

"What's the charge?"

"That I murdered him. That's all I know."

"They give you bail?"

"$100,000. I don't have that money."

"What about your husband, Lucy?"

"We haven't been together in years. I don't have anything, Jack. I really need your help."

"Don't talk with anyone until you get a lawyer. They probably have a public defender in the county. Tell them you need a public defender. I'm surprised they didn't offer you one already."

"Jack, would you come to help me?" She asked, pleading.

"I don't know if I can Lucy. Let me call you back. Sit tight, Lucy, I'll get back to you tomorrow morning. Just remember, no talking to anyone."

"Thank you so much, Jack. I knew I could count on you."

Actually, Jack couldn't count on Lucy. She'd dumped him for Steve Andros during his second year of college, when he'd shown up at her house and she unceremoniously announced she was seeing another guy. Jack was devastated, took a long time to get over her, well until after he'd moved to Galesburg for the last two years of college. In a sense he'd never gotten over her, as they say you never get over your first love.

Jack knew that Lucy had slowly drifted downhill in the years since they had been an item, drinking and attaching herself to men who could only be characterized as less than ambitious, and that was being charitable. She'd married a guy named Rafe Wetterau.

He dialed a friend in Chicago with whom he'd attended law school, got the name of an attorney in Quincy, Leon Burnside. He phoned him, telling him of their common connection with the Loyola friend, explained the call from Lucy.

"You mind meeting her up in Carthage? I'll pay you for your time. I just need you to give me the lay of the land, that's all. She'll probably be getting a public defender."

He called Lucy, told him that Burnside would be up to see her the next day, that he needed an attorney to get all the details of the case. "Lucy, this guy isn't going to be your attorney, but I need one to interview you."

"I'll be in touch," he said.

Lucy Tozzini. Sometimes you hear a name from the past and it all comes racing back, as if no time at all had passed. His brain synapses were processing files way back in his brain that had been imprinted years ago but dusty from disuse. Wild times on the river, drinking with friends out in small clearings in the corn fields on hot summer nights, laughing your ass off at silly-ass stuff, and very much in love as only an 18-year-old can be. He could even recall the smells and sounds of those nights, the way the sky looked and how the cooler air would take over the night from the hot day.

His other friends from those years had left the county, just as Jack had. Louis Devereux, his best buddy, the one who sliced his leg open on the river, was a doctor at the Mayo Clinic in Minnesota, the father of four sons, a successful oncologist. They spoke with one another twice a year, on their birthdays. They'd speak for maybe five minutes and then the conversation would peter out mainly because the two had gone such different ways and their friendship was one of only shared experiences long ago, not an organic one that refreshes itself every time you get together to talk.

Mary Devore had left Carthage for Wyoming after college, married a rancher. He'd lost touch with her long ago, saw a picture of her on Facebook and it looked like she had maintained her girl-next-door looks. She was the wild one, the one who was always drinking and carousing when they were in high school. Because she looked so squeaky-clean people thought she was the goody-two-shoes but she was the one who got drunk the most and played around with a lot of guys. She obviously had settled down and met a very wealthy man. Carol Stebbins wasn't so lucky. She was the quiet one, with a great sense of humor and got the best grades of all of them. She had moved to St. Louis and begun a career in advertising but got uterine cancer and died at 35, leaving a husband and two kids behind. Steve Finnegan left for parts unknown when they were in their twenties, last anyone heard he was living as a hermit in Hawaii, a victim of some sort of mental illness. Cadge Lavery was killed by a drunk driver in Missouri when he was only 21.

And then there was Lucy. Everybody liked Lucy, she was the one who everyone felt the most comfortable with. She never made you feel stupid or nerdy or out of place like so many kids feel at that age. She just enjoyed everyone's company and they did hers.

Seven of us, a tight little group at one time in Carthage. Two down, five to go.

CHAPTER 9

LUCY WETTERAU

The chirping of the cicadas in the trees along the river used to calm me down like nothing else. Their rhythm was so regular I could fall asleep to the soothing sound. Jack and I were lying on a blanket on the big berm on the river that the Corps of Engineers had built a couple of years ago to keep the floodwaters from overflowing into the county. We were both looking up at the sky, talking about what we wanted to do with our lives. I can even remember what the sky looked like that day, actually it was sunset and the clouds were wispy and way up high, just thin little strips that had gone red from the reflection of the setting sun. Jack turned to me and we kissed, real soft like, and then we looked at the sky again. It was so peaceful.

Jack for sure wanted the get out of Hancock County but he didn't think his family had the money to get him into a college or even over to Champaign. Me? Well, I just wanted to keep hanging out with Jack forever. Truth be told I didn't think about the future that much, never was a person to dwell too much on what my plans might be up ahead.

My mom told me to forget about school, I'd have to keep working to help support myself and my younger brother who was born with Down's Syndrome. My dad had left us years ago and we hadn't heard from him since although one of the guys at the junkyard said he'd heard my dad was with a woman who used to hang out at one of the bars in Hamilton and they were somewhere in Iowa near Des Moines. I don't even remember much about him because I was pretty small when he left. All I really recall was him and my mother yelling.

I was crazy about Jack, and I knew he loved me. We'd been running around for about a year, just about every night. When he got out of the ValuRite he'd come over to the DariBar and wait for me to get out of work. We'd race off to see our friends, maybe get a little drunk or smoke some weed, go out in the country and have a party, spread out blankets next to a cornfield. We'd all be there, Lou and Mary – they were an item, and Carol and Steve and Cadge.

I loved the way Jack held me, so tender. Never had a man hold me that way since then. There were times when I'd be with some guy and think hey this guy can't hold a candle to Jack. I wish he were back here with me, hold me like he used to. We had a real thing going then and it made me so happy.

That fall Jack went up to Spoon River and we didn't get to see each other as much. I kept working at the DariBar, but then got a second job at the HandyDandy Laundramat. I met Steve Andros there. He was a good looking guy and he never stopped pestering me for a date. Why I ever agreed to go out with him is still a mystery to me, maybe just to stop him pestering me. I thought maybe it would be one date and that would be it. What harm could that do?

But I went out more than once with him. It may have been more serious on his part than mine but Steve did some things that I thought then were pretty exciting. We did some cocaine, we had sex like I'd never had it before with Jack. I was so stupid. But it was my own damn fault that I told Jack I was going out with Steve Andros. I should have kept that quiet. I could tell right then and there that I'd broken his heart. I could see it in his face, and the way he looked at me and the way he tried to talk to me about it. Even when he walked away I could see how crushed he was.

If I could turn back the clock to just one day it'd be that day I told Jack I was seeing Steve. I would have never opened my mouth, hugged him for dear life and never thought of Steve Andros again. Well, you never get that kind of chance to go back to that one day that may have set your life onto a different, better direction. I sometimes wondered what would have happened if I'd either never gone out with Steve Andros or if I'd never told Jack about it. Would I be living in some nice house somewhere with kids all around, happy and content, and we'd have dinner together in the candlelight and drink some wine?

Steve and I went out for about six months and it didn't go so well. We got high almost every night either on coke or weed, getting drunk too. We fought, too, sometimes him slapping me around, knocking me down a couple of times. Finally I just had enough and stopped seeing him. But I kept the cocaine habit. That was the only thing he left me with.

I'd see Jack around town every once in a while but we didn't look at each other. I'd heard from friends that he was still missing me, but I was too ashamed to even say anything. In my heart I didn't think it would do any good to go right up to him and apologize, sure he'd just turn away and make me feel even worse than I did. Why did I not just go right up to him and say I made a big mistake and beg him to have me back?

Time just sort of passed by, my mom getting sicker and sicker each day because of her drinking, my brother wondering what happened to momma. I tried my best to take care of him, but I was so busy with jobs and doing drugs that I couldn't look after him very well. One day somebody from the department of family services came and took him away, saying the house was unfit for human habitation. My mom screamed at the poor guy who had come to the house but he was just doing his job. The house was a pig-sty, my mom drunk all day, lying on the couch smoking cigarettes. I can remember to this day the smell in that house, a combination of shit, rotting food and cigarette smoke.

By that time Jack had gone away up to Galesburg at Knox College and I never saw him except for a few times over the next couple of years. We still didn't look at each other. Somebody told me that he was going out with a girl up there, and I was happy for him. Me? I still looked pretty good, but I was losing weight, didn't look like the girl I did in high school. I think it may have been the drugs I was doing that made we lose weight.

That's when I started going out with a lot of different guys. Some of them even paid me, but I never thought of myself as a whore. Mostly it was just blow jobs, quickies in a car or somebody's house. I needed the money for cocaine, and that was the only way I could figure how to get it. I lost my job at the laundromat when they caught me stealing quarters from the machines. By that time my mom was so sick she was pretty much in the hospital full time, her stomach about as big as a belly could get. The doctors said it was cirrhosis of the liver and that she didn't have long to live. They were right, momma passing away just near Thanksgiving. I saw my brother every once in a while, but he died too about five years later. They'd put him in this home near Springfield and that's where he ended up living, and dying. I think he died that early because he had no one in his life, and had been taken away to a strange place and momma wasn't around anymore. I went to his funeral – there were only a few people there – and he's buried in a small cemetery next to the place he lived in Springfield.

CHAPTER 10

JACK LAPOINT

My firm has defended hundreds of clients charged with every conceivable crime from rape to embezzlement, murder to malpractice. My win rate is about fifty/fifty, which is pretty good for a defense attorney. My win rate in front of a jury is about seventy-five percent, which is out of the ballpark. Most cases got pled down, dropped, or the defendant decides to tell the truth and plead guilty. It never ceases to amaze me that so many defendants fight and fight charges, then in the end, just before trial, get cold feet and throw in the towel. But then again I've never been charged with a crime so I don't know firsthand what it does to you emotionally. The legal system grinds people down so maybe they just figure it's easier to surrender in the end.

Most people assume that if someone is charged with a crime there's a very good chance they're guilty. Wrong. A lot of innocent people are charged with crimes. And prosecutors and cops are far from perfect, far from the stereotypes portrayed on television. Like many lawyers they're venal, ambitious, malicious, mendacious, anything you can dream up. Every once in a while I come across a decent prosecutor with a conscience, but it isn't often. With those good types I know they eventually become defense attorneys or leave the law business altogether. Actually, a lot of lawyers leave the business all the time. They get into real estate, or insurance, or something completely different like manufacturing or even get another degree in counseling. I've known a couple of lawyers who switched and went to medical school and became doctors.

Also, prosecutors arrest people all the time for nefarious reasons. Sometimes they use a charge as a wedge to have the suspect turn on someone else, or there's political pressure to arrest somebody, anybody. Judges, too, are often stupid, vain, ignorant, imperious. This is probably true of a lot of professions. My friend Barney tells me that in his field, medicine, there are doctors who are butchers, sadists and sociopaths.

I see myself as the guy who levels the playing field. Probably half the people I defend are likely guilty, half either innocent or not guilty of the specific charge that they're facing. I do believe down to the bottom of my soul that everyone should have the right to legal representation, whether they can afford it or not. I really believe that you are innocent until proven guilty, although most people just assume that if you're charged you're guilty. That doesn't mean you have to like all your clients, but you have to do your best on their behalf.

Some clients I hate, others I like quite a bit. I like Cornelius Bonomono, and I like Bradford Spellman, who was accused of murdering his business partner, or at least hiring someone to do it. I suspect Bradford actually did hire the killer, but never was sure one way or the other. Brad is a sphinx, an enigma. The case against him failed because the prosecution did a shitty job and I exploited the hell out of that. I convinced the jury that any number of people could have had his partner killed because his partner was really a bad guy who pissed off a lot of people. I think that may have really been the way it happened.

There are some clients who are vermin, people I know are born criminals. Sometimes I'd try to foist them off on my partners, but they are hip to my tricks and turn me down. But, guilty or not guilty, they all have to pay. Crime always pays for us attorneys. I've never felt guilty about making money this way. I provide a very necessary service, at times a very important service. A lot of people carp and moan about attorneys but I can tell you right off that if you're in serious trouble with the law you will do anything you can to get the very best lawyer, and they're always worth the money.

Then there was Marvin Wheelock. He's evil, in a class of his own. He scared the shit out of me. He had been charged in a double murder, and my first meeting with him was chilling. "You the attorney who's going to get me out of this," he asked me, and he had a big sneer on his face. "I'm as innocent as the day I was born." I physically edged my chair even further away from him at the conference table when I heard that.

Wheelock killed a husband and wife with his bare hands. His defense was paid for by a wealthy brother from Hingham who was convinced Marvin was innocent.

The jury didn't feel quite the same way about this monster, whose malevolence oozed out across the courtroom floor, despite Marvin being decked out in a thousand-dollar suit. My theatrical tricks couldn't hide the fact that he was evil. Truth be told I throttled back on his defense, pulled my punches. Wheelock got a life sentence, thank God. I was just sorry that Marvin hadn't committed his crime in Missouri, where they wouldn't have thought twice about sending him down to Potosi to face the needle. Although Massachusetts doesn't have a death penalty, I'm one of those who feel it should have one. I've been around enough evil creatures that I think we should just remove them from this earth. I don't tell any of my liberal friends this, though. Maybe if they came face to face with that Wheelock guy they'd feel different about that.

Juries are all over the map, unpredictable, like untethered bottle rockets on the Fourth of July. Lawyers who say they can predict verdicts are full of shit. Good juries watch everything, pay attention to every detail and are still capable of horribly wrong-headed verdicts. The converse is true as well, twelve morons reaching new heights in jurisprudence. I never get hung up on all the fuss defense attorneys and prosecutors make about jury selections. They overthink it do death, wondering if they have enough women on the jury, or men, or African Americans, or young people or old people. My theory is people mostly think for themselves and it doesn't really make much difference who is on a jury, I'm confident I can make my case to anyone. A lot of lawyers disagree with me, but my success rate is pretty good.

Everything matters in a jury trial. The look of the defendant, the attitude of the judge, the prosecutor's attire. The facts are paramount of course, but even facts are sifted through the gimlet eyes of the jury members. Juries can be spiteful, racist, vengeful, good-hearted, dense, or merciful. Some know immediately if they are being played by either the prosecutor or the defense attorney. It's dangerous to overplay your hand, or underplay it. I don't try to overthink a jury, more like roll with it, gently ride and glide it toward my direction. Every trial is a totally new dynamic and all I have is a big bag of tricks in which to reach in and hope for the best. Much of a trial's progress is like a strategy I learned playing tennis, just keep hitting the ball over the net and let your opponent make mistakes by hot-dogging and grand-standing.

Here's my secret to success. As long as you're likeable, a good guy, without pretensions or airs about you, people cut you a lot of slack. People don't make judgements based on facts, statistics, raw data – they make decisions based on impressions, feelings, instinct and intuition. It's the way we're built. Even people who think they're very rational in their decision-making, people like engineers or scientists, usually make their decisions based upon a lot of emotional components. Ask really good salesmen what makes people tick and they'll tell you this is true.

It's hard, too, to tell whether someone is lying. Many in the legal profession say they can do it, but I think it's mostly empty talk. Some people lie so well because in their hearts they've convinced themselves they're telling the truth. People telling the truth can look like they're lying, and vice versa. The only clue that I pay attention to, and it's a crude one, is that nervous people are often telling the truth, calm ones often lying. But that can be deceptive, too, so I guess I really can't tell myself.

The other thing I believe in is that nothing is what it seems, there's always more to a story. It's not always because people lie, which they do, but because there's just too many moving parts in play at all times, too many things to know, little pieces that get lost, ignored, bypassed. The truth with a capital "T" is something that we may discover after we die but while we're living it's the shadow slipping away in a dark alley, elusive, a vapor.

The lawyer I hired in Quincy called me after his meeting with Lucy. It didn't look good for her. She'd been arrested at the man's house, her prints were on the knife used to kill him. It wasn't even clear whether this guy Eddie Crane was her boyfriend or not, but they did have a relationship of some sort. He told me that she was confused, but he couldn't tell if she was being evasive or just upset and scared. He learned from the state's attorney that Lucy had his blood on her when the sheriff's deputies arrived and that someone else called 911 but they didn't know who. Lucy also had a long history of drug and alcohol abuse. I asked him if he thought Lucy did it, but he said it was hard to tell because he thought she acted like someone who's innocent, confused to beat the band and bewildered. Maybe she was in a drug stupor when she did it, he speculated. He thought the evidence against her was strong, but not bulletproof.

He said that the public defender's office in Hancock County was just one woman and she was inexperienced. This didn't bode well for Lucy as public defenders are usually the lowest on the food chain, sometimes just has-been hacks who drink too much or newbie lawyers who stay in the job a year and can't wait to run for the hills. I couldn't imagine what kind of public defender worked in Hancock County, which is really a backwater.

I looked at the county's website and saw the Wakefield Cole Jr., was the state's attorney. The site didn't even give his credentials. Well, maybe he was an incompetent, too. There wasn't any information on the public defender.

CHAPTER 11

BRADFORD SPELLMAN

I never thought it would be as easy as it turned out to be but thank God in the end that someone had told me about Jack LaPoint. Marcus and I had started out as pretty good business partners in the IT business when things were just taking off in Boston. We started a little company out on Route 128 helping companies put together their computer systems and it grew like a weed for the first five years until we had about 150 employees and we were making so much money we didn't even know how to spend it all. I had more than two millions dollars in investments before I was 35 years old.

The huge success we had sort of drove Marcus and me apart. He started to do weird things like buying a house he didn't need, going on trips to Asia that he called vacations but were these sex tours where he'd be with two or three teenage girls at a time. He started to do cocaine and he was unfocused and not tending to the business. I was doing all the work keeping things going, which you have to do with a company that big. I had a bunch of talks with him but he didn't seem to be listening. We fought a few times and things went downhill after that. He was like a different person. He even did drugs in his office, and I caught him one time snorting coke off his desk.

I met with our attorneys and accountants and tried to figure out how we could build a firewall between Marcus and the corporation, and we managed to keep him from accessing some of the money for his wild lifestyle, which I thought had really gotten out of hand. He seemed to be addicted to everything. I'd never seen any of this coming in the early days when we worked so hard to get the company up and running.

I had to get him out of the company somehow and then an idea came into my head that maybe I could hire somebody to hurt him, maybe put him out of commission for a time as I moved him out of the company altogether. At first I thought that was the stupidest idea and thought of it as mostly a fantasy. But then things got worse with Marcus and he was starting to imperil the company with his behavior – clients were starting to notice and they were getting skittish. Then the idea of doing something drastic to get him out of the way wasn't so far-fetched.

I started to think how does someone go about doing something like that – hurting a guy -- and how can you go about doing it in such a way that no one would ever see your tracks?

I figured you had to build a bunch of firewalls between me and whoever eventually did the dirty work. I had a friend who knew a few guys in Chelsea who did less than savory things. I asked innocently where those guys hung out. What happened is that it went through channels. One guy talked to another guy, and I had deniability about the whole thing. Money was passed along.

Like so many things in business, and in life, wires get crossed and things get fucked up in translation, especially as the message gets passed along verbally from one guy to the next. I didn't want Marcus killed, only hurt bad enough to get him out of the picture long enough that I could get him out of the company. I was thinking maybe a broken leg or something, and I told this to the first guy I talked to about this.

It didn't turn out that way. One day the cops called me and said that Marcus had been found dead at his house, two .22 rounds to the back of the head. I was truly shocked and that came through to the cops and I wasn't even a suspect for a long time.

Eventually, though, the cops arrived at my office and arrested me. I had seen enough television shows to know that once you're arrested you don't say a thing and that you lawyer up right away and get the best attorney money can buy.

I'd heard about Jack LaPoint from one of my buddies downtown and I hired him to represent me. Funny thing is that at first I thought maybe I made a mistake hiring him because he didn't seem very smart, didn't ask me many questions, just sort of sat at his desk, every once in a while looking out the window at the harbor or something. He didn't even say much, just said thanks for the information and let's set up another meeting in a couple of days. I thought what the hell kind of hot-shot attorney is this, he didn't even get very excited?

I found out later that was Jack's style, to think first and then come up with a solution. I never let on that I was the least bit guilty in all of this, and I never could figure out if he believed me or not, but we got along pretty well. We even shared a laugh or two as we got ready for my trial.

The long and short of it was that Jack did a superb job defending me. He tore the prosecution apart and I don't think they knew what hit them. I think their mistake was to go into the case sure as shit that they had me so they stumbled all over themselves when Jack hit them hard on some key points. They had some inexperienced prosecutors working for them and the investigation got screwed up at some of the critical points and Jack made every one of the witnesses look shady and shifty. It was actually fun to watch.

He got the jury to think that Marcus had brought this all on himself, with Jack painting a scenario where Marcus had gotten in some deep trouble with bad guys and they were just getting back at him. Marcus was easy to destroy in court by all sorts of inferences because he was so fucked up to begin with and did do a lot of shady things. I never felt too guilty about the whole thing because I never hired anybody to kill him, only to hurt him a little. I couldn't be responsible for what actually happened. They never did find out who killed Marcus and I hadn't ratted anyone out because I had nobody to rat out, I was clean through the whole process. The whole thing to mess Marcus up went through intermediaries and the prosecution got it all screwed up anyway.

I paid $15,000 to have Marcus hurt, and more than $250,000 to Jack LaPoint to get me off scot-free. The company was still going gangbusters, so that was practically nothing – maybe a month's salary for me.

CHAPTER 12

LUCY WETTERAU

After my mom died, I was completely on my own. The house was never ours anyway and I didn't know where I was going to live, I couldn't afford the rent. That's when I found Rafe Wetterau, a nice guy from up around Bluffton who I met through some friends.

Rafe was a good guy, nice to me, nicer than the other guys who just wanted sex and then left me behind when they got what they wanted. Rafe moved to Carthage, and asked me to move in with him. I thought maybe now was my chance to start over again. I can't say I was wild in love with him, but I liked him and thought he treated me right.

I got clean of cocaine, although I still did a little bit of drinking. Not much, just on weekends. Rafe and I had some good times, riding around in his convertible during the summer, hanging out with friends in town. By this time Jack was in Chicago, someone told me he'd enrolled in law school. In a way I was proud of him, knowing he would make a success of himself. He was always so smart.

Rafe and I eventually got married. It wasn't anything fancy, just at the courthouse. Life was pretty good, Rafe working down at the machine shop on Curtis Avenue, me at the Burger King. We were married for maybe five year but we slowly drifted apart, mainly because I was pretty clean, and Rafe drinking pretty much every night. One night he hit me a couple of times and I said that was it, packed my bags and moved in with a friend over in Hamilton.

I kind of bounced around from job to job over in Hamilton, lived with a girlfriend for about a year and went to the bars a few nights a week. I wasn't drinking a whole lot but I was clean of cocaine and was getting bored. I needed a man in my life.

I met a guy in Hamilton named Strom Cobini, and we started going out. He seemed like a nice guy. We hung out together for about six months and then he told me he was headed out to Denver to take a job with an oil company. He asked me to go with him and I did, us traveling in his old car out there. We got a small dumpy apartment in downtown Denver. He'd go to work every day, made some pretty good money. I was a waitress at a Waffle House.

I got pregnant and Strom went nuts when he heard the news. He said he wasn't ready to be a father, and why hadn't I taken precautions in the first place? I had, but somehow I still got pregnant. He got real sullen on me in the next few months, sometimes ignoring me altogether. He wanted me to get rid of the baby, have an abortion, but I really didn't want to, I was so excited to be having a baby.

I got real big, but I'd always been strong so I was able to get around pretty good. I worked at the Waffle House until I was so big I couldn't navigate between the tables.

I was seeing a doctor and he said everything looked good, that I should be able to have the baby the regular way. I was about two weeks from my due date and I went to see the doctor for a regular appointment. When he examined me he told me and the nurse that he couldn't get a heartbeat and they rolled a bunch of machines into the room. They rushed me over to the hospital which was just across the street and delivered the baby by caesarian. My baby was dead, just lying there. I thought my life had ended, too.

Strom never even came to the hospital. I named the baby April, just like the month. She was a beautiful baby, with golden hair.

The doctor must have taken pity on me, said that he could arrange for a funeral for April over at this big Catholic cathedral near the hospital. Although I'm not Catholic, I said okay, just so April gets a funeral. Some of the nurses and doctors came to the funeral, which was very nice. The priest said some prayers, and they buried little April in a cemetery out in a place called Littleton. They even paid for the funeral and a small headstone. They were awful nice to me.

One of the nurses said she knew of a place that would take me in, she said I shouldn't ever go back to a man who wouldn't even show up for me at the hospital. I remember that nurse really well, she was a beautiful woman with huge breasts and blond hair and blue eyes and spoke with one of those English accents, although I never asked her where she was from. "That prick," she kept saying whenever she spoke of Strom.

The place she told me about was a house in town that took in abused women. Although Strom never abused me except for a few times he slapped me, I knew I never was going to go back to him and I never did see him again. Those nurses were like angels sent from heaven to help me out.

CHAPTER 13

SARAH HOLLINGSWORTH

On Fridays Jack left the downtown office early, stuffed papers in his briefcase and headed up to Lake Sunapee in New Hampshire, about a two-hour drive northwest of Boston. He'd bought the place about ten years ago in a fire sale from a client, probably at a third of what its value was today. Sarah Hollingsworth usually met him on Saturday morning, after her shift was over at Boston Children's Hospital.

Sarah and he had been seeing each other for about a year after they'd met at a party on the Back Bay. She'd been divorced, too, for about as long as Jack, and she wasn't interested in any long-term affair, certainly not marriage. Neither was he. It wasn't just about sex, either. They had fun together just the way it was, spending weekends on Lake Sunapee, going out to dinner in Newport or Keene on Saturday night, lounging around till late Sunday evening when both returned to Boston.

"What you thinking about Jack?" Sarah asked him while they were both in his boat on the lake. "You look pensive."

He told her about the call he'd had from Lucy, how she'd been charged with murder. "Can't understand how she would have gotten herself involved in such a thing."

"You know how life is, things just start and then they sometimes get out of control. Damn if I can figure how people get in the fixes they do," she said.

Sarah was a pediatric intensive care nurse, old by the standards of her co-workers, burnout being after about five years. What kept her going in such an environment was a mystery to Jack. He hated hospitals anyway, avoided them at all costs. How she could work in the belly of the beast 40 hours a week was a mystery to him.

As he looked at Sarah sitting in the prow of the boat he was reminded of the forays he made with Lucy on the Mississippi, her in the two-piece bathing suit, sultry as could be. And then he was reminded of the time they'd found the body, bloated and pale and fish-belly white, rising from the dark waters of the slough.

"We found a body once," he said.

"You what?" she asked.

"We found a body. This girl Lucy and me. We were on the river. It was a hot summer day and we found a body attached to a rope that had gotten tangled in the propeller. They never found out who it was, just a man who had drowned somewhere. The river washed the body down from somewhere up north of where we found him."

"Ooooo. That sounds spooky," she said. "What did you do?"

"We got the cops, they came up in a boat and removed the body. They said he drowned. That was pretty much it. One thing I recall was that the guy was naked, except he still had his shoes and socks on. No pants, no underwear, nothing…except shoes. How does that happen, where you lose your pants but your shoes are still on, shoestrings tied and everything?"

"Beats me," she answered. "Maybe he went in naked."

That Sarah, always thinking.

The next day the lawyer from Quincy called Jack.

"Your friend attacked one of the deputies last night. The sheriff called me this morning. She used a filed-down toothbrush handle and jabbed it in the deputy's leg. Not a bad wound, but bad enough."

"They said she was raving about something when she did it. She's been sedated in her cell. They got a 24-hour watch on her."

CHAPTER 14

CORNELIUS BONOMONO

We should have never let that asshole Ricky Moran in our little operation we had planned. Jimmy Cochran and me we had a good thing going that very few people knew about. It was all about pineapples believe it or not and it was making us some good money. Somehow Jimmy got ahold of this guy who had a deal with another guy in South America who brought in shiploads of pineapples into the country. Jimmy was one of those really cagey guys who always had something cooking and how he worked this out I have no idea, but I didn't ask many questions because he was also the kind of guy who always gave you vague answers to questions. Okay by me because Jimmy had never done anything wrong by me, and I trusted him. I shouldn't have trusted Ricky Moran, but sometimes you just never go with your instincts.

Well, anyway this pineapple thing involved offloading about two containers from a ship every Wednesday before they reached customs and we'd sell them to vendors around the city at about half the price of regular pineapples. It was all cash. It was a smooth operation and no one was the wiser and I learned a whole lot about the pineapple business in the meantime, which was very interesting to me. We'd split the proceeds with Jimmy taking a bigger share because he put the whole thing together.

As I said Jimmy had all sorts of crazy schemes going on all the time. He really was one of those Irish loonies, but he was fun to work with. It was really just Jimmy and me in the pineapple business, but then Jimmy comes up with another plan to make really big money and he wants to include Ricky Moran in on the deal because he says Ricky can help out in getting some connections we'd need for this operation. Jimmy found out that there was this company in Boston that auctioned off coin collections from around the world, really big stuff that sells for millions of dollars with gold and silver coins and such. He found out that before their big auctions they store all the coins in one place getting them ready for the showing the day before the auction. Jimmy said that's the time when all this stuff is at its most vulnerable, and there's an hour or two when nothing is under lock and key and that's the time to go in and take most of it, or at least a lot of it. Jimmy figured that if we do it we can split up maybe $4 million. Jimmy would take $2 million and I'd get $1.5 million and Ricky would get the rest.

That sounds great to me because a million I could put away and then Tony and Mary and me would have a big nest-egg stashed away somewhere for college and our retirement and stuff like that.

We spent about two months planning this operation and we had it down to the second about what everyone was supposed to do, where we were going to hit, who was going to do exactly what. We were going to wear masks, and had our escape all planned. At about six in the morning on the day we had planned to hit this office where the coins were kept we got together, and started the operation. It went great, we got into the building and all the coins were in front of us and there must have been thousands of them. The place was pretty dark so we worked in the dark. Then, out of the blue a door opens and there's this security guard standing there just sort of dumbstruck, he can't figure out what's going on, but he pulls his gun and starts to yell. That's when that fuckhead Ricky pulls a gun and shoots the guard right off and the guy falls backwards, but he gets back up and shoots back and wings Jimmy right in the shoulder. Then the guard unloads his gun and Ricky shoots the guy dead. Then I see Ricky aim the gun at me and he pulls the trigger, the bullet crashing through a cabinet I was standing by. Before I could think I shoot Ricky. I was never good with a gun but for some reason the bullet hits him right in the head and he goes down, and I'm sure he's dead.

Me and Larry hightail it out of there, not taking anything with us, figuring the gunshots alerted everybody within about two blocks. We get the hell out of that part of the city. I got Jimmy all fixed up with some bandages and stuff and his wound wasn't bad. Fortunately the police never found out who tried to rob the place, except for Ricky, which was a good thing because with the guard dead it would have been murder. They never connected Ricky with us because we'd never worked with him before. After that Jimmy and me kind of split up and even the pineapple thing fell apart when the big boys in the mob found out how much money we were making and they moved in on us and pushed us out of the way.

This happens all the time, somebody figures an angle and starts to milk it for money and if it's a success the big boys step in and move you aside. If you don't move aside they kill you.

I still had my regular job and the family and with some other action on the side we were making enough money to do pretty well, but then Mary got pregnant again and we had another one on the way and I needed to bump up my income to make way for a bigger family. Of course word got around that I had shot Ricky Moran but Jimmy squared it with the Irish guys by backing me up and telling them that Ricky tried to kill me first. Turns out that a lot of the Irish guys didn't like Ricky Moran much anyway, so everything was okay with those guys, in fact a couple of them even came up to me later and said I did everybody a favor. I could never figure out why Ricky tried to kill me, maybe it went all the way back to when I flattened him in the football game. Who knows? Another thing that was bothering me was the fact that I had killed a guy, even though it was a shitbum like Ricky Moran. I was raised a Catholic and knew it was a mortal sin to kill anyone, and I had some trouble coping with that, even though I had to do it. I figured finally that if he had killed me then Tony and Mary and our new baby wouldn't have a dad and a husband, and they'd be in really big trouble then. After figuring that out I felt better about the whole deal.

A guy from Sonny Ianetta's gang came up to me one day and offered me a job doing some work for them down at the docks making sure everything ran according to Sonny's orders. Sonny pretty much ran the docks in Boston at that time and I said what the hell, I need the extra money so I said yes. The guy that hired me was almost as big as me, and I had heard that he had a reputation as a guy who did some of Sonny's dirty work, meaning getting rid of people when the need came up. His name was Jimmy Tracadora and I made sure to stay on his good side, I didn't want any trouble from a guy like that. I'd see Jimmy Cochran every once in a while but we weren't doing any work together anymore although we stayed pretty good friends.

CHAPTER 15

CARLA COLLINS PORTER

Murders are relatively uncommon, although most Americans think they're commonplace, certainly because of the proliferation of cop shows that feature good-looking cops running to the scene, throwing all their efforts and officers at the crime, solving it by the end of the show.

That's pure baloney. Murders are extremely rare, except within certain zip codes in large cities where the illegal drug trade flourishes. In nice areas of cities, and certainly in most of the suburbs and small towns, murder is so rare as to be almost non-existent.

And when murders do happen, most of them are solved quickly because the killer either confesses or sometimes never even leaves the scene of the crime. Those murders would fill up only about three minutes of a television show. Crimes of passion resolve themselves quickly. That's it.

In other cases, unlike television, police almost always bungle either everything, or at the least a major part of the investigation. Police are stupid, or lazy, or just too busy with other cases. Clues go unnoticed, potential witnesses forgotten, phone calls ignored. Police agencies don't talk to each other, cops jump to conclusions, eye-witnesses get it all fucked up. It's simply by accident that some cases get solved at all.

Jack and his partners had seen just about every iteration of fuck-ups by police and prosecutors. Unless they had Lucy on three different videos killing this guy with a roomful of church-going old biddies watching her do it there were bound to be mistakes made. Always are. Now of course she would be facing charges of assaulting a police officer with deadly force, and there was probably a video of that.

And, you never get the full story. Not from the suspects, the police, witnesses, friends, family. Everybody either hides, shades or modifies the truth. It's a hall of mirrors. Life is a hall of mirrors.

The morning traffic to Logan Airport is always a big cluster-fuck, has been since the airport was built on landfill out in the harbor decades ago, connected to the city by tunnels underneath Boston Harbor. Even though the city spent more than 35 years and almost a trillion dollars of taxpayer money on a new tunnel system it leaks and jams up. This doesn't prevent Bostonians, the most aggressive, rude drivers outside of Mexico City, from speeding, driving on shoulders, honking horns and giving the finger. That's the one thing he really hated about Boston, alongside the Red Sox fans. He always thought that the big illuminated sign at Logan welcoming visitors to Boston should just say "Fuck You."

He really should have taken a cab but thought he'd only be away a few days, so what the hell, pay the $100-a-day airport parking fee, another great feature to Logan Airport, its hyper-inflated fees for everything. That's what happens when only two groups – Irish and Italians – run a one-party city for 100 years. Chicago was the same.

Jack had called Lucy the day before to say he'd come to Carthage and check out her situation. He was careful not to say "help" her because he didn't want to overcommit, but he knew she wasn't capable of listening to nuanced semantics.

"Thanks so much, Jack, for old times' sake," she told him.

The flight was uneventful, two hours to Chicago, then a four-hour drive to Hancock County. It had been a decade since he'd seen the place, driving in while the sunset glowed on the western horizon, open, vast.

He drove around town, passing by the house where he'd been raised, the elementary school, downtown square, beautiful four-story courthouse. He'd been right, it all looked so small now, just a few people about. Compared to Copley Square in Boston this looked so slow-moving, as if time had stopped.

He checked into the Days Inn, dumped his bags, went over to the county jail to check on Lucy.

"Lucy, we got someone to see you. Says they used to know you," a guard said.

"Jack….Jack!"

Jack was led back to the cells, told to stand behind the broad yellow line painted on the floor. "Have a seat," the guard said.

Lucy was a mess. There were tiny remnants of the young pretty woman he'd remembered, but she looked terrible, a hag, way past her years. She'd withered, sagged, her hair greasy, gray.

"Lucy, it's been such a long time, it's so good to see you again," Jack said, meaning it. "I thought it was best that I come to Carthage and find out what's happening."

She held her head in her hands, began to sob. "Jack....Jack, I don't know how this all happened. I had nothing to do with Eddie's death. I just woke up in the morning and there was blood all over. I just picked up the knife, I know I shouldn't have done that. But then the cops knocked on the door and I just answered it."

"Lucy, I'm not your attorney. Wait to tell everything to someone they appoint for you. Just keep your story to yourself until I can get this squared away."

She rose, placed her face near the bars. "Jack, it's so good to see you. You look great. I always knew that you'd make something of yourself. I knew that way back when we had so much fun. I didn't think I was good enough for you."

"We can talk later, Lucy."

The guard escorted him out.

"You here to defend her?" he asked.

"Can't say yes or no right now," Jack said.

He went to a dinner that night just outside of town, sat in a booth and thought about Lucy. And about his life as well.

The next morning he called the public defender's office. A woman answered the phone. He explained who he was, why he'd come to Carthage.

"Lucy told me you were coming," said Carla Collins Porter, the county's single public defender.

Judging by her voice on the phone – strong and sure – he was surprised when a thin, petite woman greeted him at her office on the third floor of the courthouse. Probably weighing 110 pounds, with short black hair, Carla Collins Porter had a firm handshake, an open smile. Jack judged her age in the mid to late forties. No wedding ring.

"Great to see a native son who made good," she said. "When I heard you were coming to visit Lucy I did a bit of research on you. You're the legal version of the U.S. Cavalry. Miss Wetterau is in deep trouble, as you probably know."

"Are you representing her officially?" Jack asked.

"Not yet, officially. She was waiting for you to arrive."

Porter explained that Lucy had a reputation in Hamilton as a flake, getting drunk out at the Rooster House bar on the riverfront, cozying up to men who brought her drinks. Her husband was a drunk, too, but not so bad he couldn't hold a job as a mechanic at Showalter's Ford in Carthage. They didn't live together. "I'd call him a medium-functioning drunk, not a real smart guy," she said.

"She has no history of violence, really nothing more than being a public nuisance. But the evidence is pretty strong. She's in the apartment with a dead man, his throat cut, she's standing there with the knife in her hand when the police arrive. It sounds like the opening scene of an Agatha Christie novel."

"What about the victim, any information on him?"

"He's a shit-bum," she said. Jack was surprised a woman who looked like such a delicate creature would use such a term. It sounded funny coming from her.

"He's – he was – unemployed, a druggie over in Hamilton. Worked in Nauvoo at the Mormon complex over there, but they fired him as soon as they found out about the drugs," she said.

Nauvoo was the original settlement of the Mormons, and the denomination had built a huge complex there, part museum, part shrine. It was from Nauvoo that Brigham Young left, leading the Mormons to Salt Lake City. Had Joseph Smith and his brother not been murdered in Carthage, Nauvoo would be the size of Salt Lake City.

"Do you know why the bail was set so high, especially since Lucy has no criminal background?"

"I can't figure that out, except maybe our new judge is full of herself, wants to be seen as a tough cookie. She was appointed only a year ago. Been a big pain in my ass. I'm sure there's not going to be any bail now that she stabbed the deputy."

Jack had seen his share of that type judge, small-time attorneys elevated into semi-gods drunk on their own power. Most of the time their cases get shredded by appellate courts but it creates a big mess because you have to go through all the agony of their vanity and incompetence. Then you still have to appeal.

"Should we go see Lucy?" Jack asked.

Lucy looked pathetic in the orange jumpsuit. Put that outfit on anyone – let's say the Supreme Court justices – and they'd look like shady mobsters or child-killers. Lucy was shaking, sweating, probably in the throes of withdrawal from God knows what. She could barely follow along.

"Lucy, I need you to tell me everything that happened, from the night before until the police arrived," Jack said.

"Let's see...," Lucy said, wandering off.

"Lucy! Get with it!" Carla boomed. It startled Jack, too. But it woke Lucy awake, her eyes widening.

"We need to help you, Lucy, and we can't if you keep avoiding this," Carla said.

Lucy said that she and Eddie had spent the evening before at the Owl's Nest bar in Hamilton down by the river, gotten pretty blitzed and she walked back to his apartment, Eddie stayed behind to do some more drinking with his friends. She passed out on the bed.

The next she knew it was morning and she was laid out on the floor of the bedroom, her clothes half off. She went into the front room and there he was, blood everywhere, his throat cut. She saw the knife next to him, and stupidly picked it up. A few seconds later the cops came in, having been called by somebody who thought they heard screams.

Jack's brain was already spinning with potential holes in the prosecution's case. Why would somebody have called 911 that morning when any screaming might have occurred in the middle of the night? Blood analysis may show that he was stabbed much earlier, and the blood on Lucy's hands, and the knife, were hours old. He could already see the beginnings of plausible doubt in jurors' minds.

Lucy explained that she and Eddie weren't exactly boyfriend and girlfriend, "more like fuckbuddies," she said. "It really wasn't anything serious." For some reason it hurt Jack to hear the word "fuckbuddies" come from Lucy.

"Eddie had a few problems. He didn't see so well, he was always bumping into things. Sometimes he had a hard time keeping it up, too, especially if he had too much to drink. But he was a good guy, I would have never laid a hand on him, much less cut his throat."

"Who would want him dead, Lucy?" Jack asked.

"I don't know. Eddie liked kids," Lucy said. "You know, like liked kids."

"What's that mean, Lucy, tell us," Carla said.

"He didn't do anything to them. But he filmed them."

"Filmed them doing what?" Carla asked.

"You know, doing stuff."

"What stuff?" Jack asked.

"Sex stuff."

"And you were fine with this, Lucy?" Carla asked.

"He told me he didn't do anything with the kids, he just filmed them. You got to understand that Eddie was a good guy, never did anything bad to me."

"What did he do with the films?" Carla asked.

"They weren't his films. He was just the cameraman," Lucy said.

"Who did he work for?" Carla asked

"He never said. A guy."

"Where?"

"All over."

"Where did the kids come from?"

"From other guys."

"Where?"

"All over the country."

She might be lying, Jack thought. Or maybe this Eddie had lied to her. A guy with eyes so bad he bumped into things is a cameraman? Hardly. These kinds of guys tell women all sorts of things. But why tell her something so despicable? It's not something you would naturally brag about to a woman, or anyone.

Jack had heard a lot of scuzzy stuff in his career. Not everything was true, but there didn't seem to be a bottom to the depth of human depravity. This had to rate down near whatever bottom did exist, again, if it was true, but Jack doubted it.

And this was the woman who he was crazy about thirty-some years ago, would have married had she had him.

CHAPTER 16

JACK LAPOINT

At our house we always had to have dinner together because my dad insisted on it. He also had to serve out the food, tiny portions for me, my sister and my brother. My mom said it was because my dad's family was poor and tried to get by with little. If we complained about how small the portions were he always said we could come back for more.

My mom was always trying to explain away the quirky things my father did, and he did a lot of quirky things. He always went in and out of the house through the same door, the one in back. If we all went in the side or front door, he'd walk around and go in the back door.

Actually he was a great dad, and truth be told he was more kid himself than adult. He played with us like he was a kid, too, horsing around on the floor with us when we were little kids.

I never knew why his law practice in Carthage didn't do well. He was smart, after all he'd graduated from the law school at the University of Illinois, but for some reason it never flourished. I think deep down inside he wasn't real interested in working, at least didn't need to be working all the time. He was more a thinker, enjoyed his own company, not that he didn't have friends, just that he was content to be by himself.

He could drive my mom crazy. She was the one who should have gone to law school, a sharp mind and true skeptic. I always thought she would have made a great cop, too, she could smell bullshit from a mile away. My mom was much more ambitious than my dad and that frustrated her.

They were always at odds about something but oddly enough they showed quite a bit affection for one another, sometimes embarrassing us kids. Speaking of parents embarrassing their kids with displays of affection I dated a girl in college and when I took her home one night we opened the front door and there were her parents going at it on the sofa, naked. That girl screamed, pushed me out the door and kept screaming at her parents. I thought it was hilarious, but if it had been my parents I would have thrown up right on the spot.

I came home one night after partying, half-drunk and was stripping off my clothes in the bedroom when my dad walked in on me. All he said was my mom was sick and would I sit with her while he called 911. I went in to see my mom, she was as white as a corpse, cold to the touch. I thought she was dead. The ambulance came and got her and she stayed almost a week in the hospital. It was never told to me what was wrong with her and it wasn't discussed. I learned later from my sister that my mom had had a complete nervous breakdown.

My mom was delighted when I told her I wanted to go to law school. I think she was living her life vicariously through me and she called me up every week and wanted to know my progress, what things I'd learned about the law.

Right in the middle of my second year in law school my dad had a bad stroke. He was in the hospital for ten days and never woke up. We all rotated shifts watching him 24 hours a day and I was the one on duty in the room when he died. I was watching him in the bed, and all of a sudden he jerked and I got up from the chair and went over to the bed. I looked at him and knew he had died, there was no breathing. I remember it was 1:47 in the morning when I called the nurse. She confirmed the time of death. I stared at him for just a couple of minutes but I never cried, just held his hand and said goodbye, then drove home and told my mom. I cried plenty later when I got back to Chicago after the funeral. My dad was a great guy.

Everybody always thought I was such a straight arrow but there were two things that happened in law school and right after that might have changed people's minds. I snorted cocaine every night of the week, and I cheated on my bar exam. The cocaine was kind of normal for a lot of the law students, and I'm not ashamed to say I used it. Thank God I kicked the habit shortly after graduation and I've never used it again. But the cheating is something I never told anybody about. Who would?

It wasn't a lot of cheating but it was still cheating. I had a friend whose father was in the Illinois Bar and he was one of the guys who put the test together. My friend got part of the exam, copied it from his dad's desk at home, and we worked on the answers ahead of time. I'm not sure if that's what tipped the scales in my passing, but it could have.

I'm real quiet about the fact that I also shave a few ethical corners from time to time when it serves my purpose. I feel bad about it later but it doesn't stop me from doing it anyway. I figure everybody makes compromises in their careers, and I just rack it up to that. They aren't awful things, just shortcuts when I need to get something done. I've never allowed any of my clients to outright lie in court, but sometimes I've made the truth do some pretty amazing contortions.

I have this funny thing about money. Most of the time I don't give a big shit about it, as long as I know there's always a reserve hidden somewhere. I think that might come from my childhood when things were kind of tight. I cut lawns, did odd jobs for neighbors, came up with ways to make a few bucks here and there. I had a bank account down at the First National downtown, and I'd put money into it every time I made some. I think it was my way of feeling secure. Once I started making some serious money I continued that habit, saving what I could, and stashing it away. When the really big money started coming in I had what I called my hidden stash that nobody knew about, not my wife, not my partners, not even my accountant. I kept that stuff in a safe deposit box, some of it in cash, other things like gold coins. I'd put things in there a little at a time, just in case there came a time I might need it, my own little fund, although the last time I checked it wasn't so little. It was just like when I was a kid.

Everybody has their own view of money, and how they handle it, or don't handle it, is one key to knowing their personality. Some of my friends are cheap as hermits even though they have tons of money, others spend like there's no tomorrow, even though they don't have that much to begin with. Watch what happens when a big check is put on the table when you're in a restaurant. Some pick it right up, others look at it as if it's a poisonous snake. That gives you all you need to know about how they feel about money.

CHAPTER 17

JACK LAPOINT/CARLA COLLINS PORTER/LUCY WETTERAU

After Jack and Carla Collins Porter had interviewed Lucy both headed back to the courthouse.

"Can I use your office?" Jack asked, "I've got some calls I need to return."

"Go ahead, we can talk later. I've got some things I need to take care of too," Carla answered.

Her office, although small, was surprisingly plush for a county office, located as it was in a corner of the third floor two doors down from the courtroom. A huge old desk from which she obviously worked, piled high with papers. Jack preferred an immaculate desk so it didn't intimidate him every time he walked into his office, remind him of how much work that awaited him each day. He noticed, too, that she had no framed diplomas on her wall. It was standard procedure for attorneys to festoon their walls with diplomas and certificates. Doctors did the same. The one thing that dominated the room was a beautiful copy of one of Winslow Homer's oil paintings of the Maine coast, a piece called "A Summer's Night," from a place that Jack had actually visited.

"Please, use the conference room over there. Close the door if you want privacy," she said.

"I love your desk – it's beautiful."

"Actually, it's built for two people, it's called a 'partners' desk,' people would sit facing each other." Jack had actually heard of such things, seen them in a few Boston offices. He once even bid on one at an auction but the price got too high, upwards of $10,000. Hancock County must be doing pretty well if it could provide such an office to a public defender.

"I think I'll probably be busy for the rest of the day. But I was wondering if we might be able to go to dinner tonight, discuss Lucy's case?" He went out on a limb in asking, not knowing if she was married, with a partner.

"I have yoga at five, but I could be ready by about 6:30. There's not a whole lot of good restaurants here, why don't we go over to Keokuk, there's a few good places over there right on the river."

"Good for me. Where do you want me to pick you up?"

"Oh, right here in front of the courthouse, I only live across the street. Don't believe in long commutes."

Jack picked her up at the courthouse steps promptly at 6:30. He was always on time, hated it when people were late. The lawyers at his firm understood this, having been briefed by his partners that it was the single thing that pissed him off.

Carla had obviously been wearing "work" clothes earlier, now she was much shapelier than her previous outfit let on, certainly more fashionable. Some women were pretty, others stunning or striking or sultry. Carla was cute.

"Show me the way," he said as she got into his car.

"Go west, young man, I believe you already know the territory," she said, smiling. She sat in his car like a teenage girl.

A half hour later they were at the riverfront in Keokuk, in a small Italian restaurant facing the river. It certainly wasn't up to the standards of the Italian restaurants in Boston's North End, but how could you screw up spaghetti, which actually was his favorite Italian dish, unsophisticated as he was? His friends would laugh at him when he ordered it at the plush Italian eateries in Boston, the waiters blanching when he did it. One waiter had sniffed "We don't serve spaghetti here, sir, you can get that down the street." He never went back to that place.

"So what do you think?" Carla asked.

"I think it was very lucky I never married the woman. Of course, she was the one who dumped me," Jack said, smiling.

"I'm not trying to avoid an answer, but I'll toss the question back to you. What do you think?" Jack asked.

"I think Eddie needed killing, if what she's saying is true, a jury in Hancock County might make her a special deputy for getting rid of him."

"Legally, what do you think?"

"I think she's either going to plead guilty, or be found guilty," Carla said. "She's not a very good defendant, certainly not in the state she's is now."

"I think we can find some holes in their case," he said, explaining what some of his initial ideas were for forming a defense. Carla listened closely, looking right into Jack's eyes. "Honest eyes," Jack always called them, when a person looks you straight on.

Barney Componari, a psychiatrist and good friend of Jack's, claimed that the totality of a person's face said everything about a person. "It's the soul, really, etched on the face," he told him once, explaining that the way to ascertain a person was to take in the entire face, how it worked together with the eyes, the smile, the movement of the lips, how a person held his or her head, that determined the inner personality. Jack tried to use that in determining whether or not people were sincere, telling the truth. He wasn't sure it was accurate, but he trusted Componari to know what he was talking about.

Barney had been trained at Harvard, was probably one of the best psychiatrists in Boston, but had been of late shifting more toward theology, fixated on Dante's Divine Comedy, certain it contained some elemental key to understanding life. Jack had tried to read it, found it totally impenetrable, unreadable.

"Barney, I bought a copy of the Divine Comedy, at least the Inferno part, and I can't get past page three without getting cross-eyed confused. It's like reading hieroglyphics."

"I think I can explain that, Jack," Barney had said. "It's because you're a dumbshit." He loved Barney's no-nonsense ways and his sense of humor, something usually sorely lacking in psychiatrists.

He had come across Componari in a case in which he was defending a mother who had killed her two children. "She's guilty, she knows it, she wasn't insane.

You got an uphill case with her," he had said. "This isn't a legal or medical term, but she's evil," he had added. Barney wasn't going to be any help as an expert witness. The jury agreed with Barney, put her away for life.

"I noticed you said the word "we," Jack. Does that mean you want to work on the case?" Carla asked.

That was an excellent question. Jack had tons of work awaiting him in Boston. This might be a stimulating break from the grueling legal scene he'd been in for a quarter of a century, a chance to see how small-town law worked, even a chance to get out of Boston once in a while over the next couple of weeks, rent a nice boat, fish on the Mississippi. After all, he had passed the Illinois Bar, was licensed to work in the state.

"Can I get back to you on that?

"Sure. I was just teasing you anyway. I know you're probably booked solid and this case is pretty small compared with the stuff I bet you work on all the time."

Their dinner came, a big plate of spaghetti for Jack, something much lighter for Carla. "I feel like a pig eating all of this in front of you. Want some? He asked.

"No, I'm fine with a salad," she said.

"This is why I'm probably three times your weight," he said as he dug into his spaghetti. It was delicious, better than any on the North End.

"How did you find your way to Hancock County," he asked.

"Chose it at random, actually. I went to Chicago Kent and was looking for a place where I could practice law, maybe help a few people along the way." Chicago Kent was the law school that produced a lot of the rough and tumble lawyers who constituted many of the state's attorneys in Illinois. It was a no-nonsense school, light on the theoretical, great on street-smart law. The chin-strokers went to Northwestern and the University of Chicago, the cagey street fighters went to Chicago Kent. Jack's Loyola University was somewhere between the two.

"Where are you from?"

"Grew up in Chicago, on the north side. Went to Mount Holyoke College in your home state, moved back to Chicago, got married, then got divorced. I have twin sons, both of whom are at the University of Illinois right now. Not a very dramatic story."

"I love Carthage, love the county. Funny how you can pick a place at random and it all works out," she added.

"You don't find it boring?" he asked.

"Not at all. I'm as busy as I want to be, plus I've made a few really good friends and I love the pace. My boys aren't too far away, either. I go over there, or they come here."

"What about you, Jack, tell me your story."

He explained his life in Carthage, law school in Chicago, the move to Boston, how his firm evolved from a two-bit storefront operation to the size it was now. He mentioned the two divorces, his son, what his life was like now.

"Tell me about Lucy – the Lucy you knew," she asked.

"Lucy...well it was way back in the early 80s, when we were both very young. You wouldn't know it from looking at the woman now but back then she was as sexy as they came, caught my eye from the very beginning, full of life, fun, easy to talk with. My mother thought she was beneath us, from the wrong side of the tracks as they used to say. But I was head over heels as only a 17-year-old can be, topped off with testosterone and ready to take on the world. We had a lot of fun."

"What happened?" Carla asked.

"Like I said, she dumped me. There was another guy. Thank God for small favors."

"Would you like to go on the river Saturday?" Jack asked, out of the blue.

"What?"

"Want to go on the river? I don't have to be back until Sunday night. I could rent a boat and we could make a day of it, assuming the weather holds out."

"Hmmm…well, I've got my gardening class in the morning, but I might be able to skip it. I usually go into work in the afternoon, but I can put that off, too…yeah, that sounds fun."

The next day they met with Lucy again. She still looked like shit, but at least was following the conversation.

"Lucy, tell us again about Eddie and the films," Carla opened. "We need to know the whole story."

"Well, he told me that he was making these films, sometimes doing it in Hamilton, sometimes Chicago, sometimes St. Louis. Some guys would get the kids, and he'd film them doing stuff."

"You said Eddie had poor eyesight. How could he be filming if he couldn't see?" Jack asked.

"Well, he said he actually helped, with the lighting and stuff."

"Did you ever see any of these films?"

"Oh God, no. I wouldn't watch something like that."

"Why did you hang around this guy after you found this out?"

"He was good to me. He gave me drugs, we had a good time together."

"Did he work? I mean did he work doing anything besides those films?" Carla asked.

"Well he worked over at Nauvoo, with the Mormons, but they let him go."

"Why?"

"I think they found out he was drinking too much, or something like that. Maybe he was late for work a few times. They're a bunch of holier-than-thou pricks over there."

"Did you know his friends?"

"There was a guy named Billy, and a guy named Buster. I remember thinking 'Billy and Buster,' two bees."

"You don't remember waking up even once during that night after you passed out. How did you get on the floor? Why were half of your clothes off when you woke up? Which half?"

"Bottom half."

"Your panties, too?"

"I think so."

"You can't remember having panties on or off?" Carla asked, incredulous.

"I was so drunk, I can't remember."

"Did you two have sex of any kind?"

"No. Not that I remember."

"Did you have intercourse?"

"Not that I know."

"You couldn't tell?" Carla asked.

"Didn't see any sperm or anything down there."

The interview went on for another half hour. As the two left the jail they looked at one another.

"No way she can go on the stand. She's half-crazy. She might be guilty as sin," Carla said.

"Might be, but the story always changes a dozen times before you go to trial," he said.

"By the way, you get a boat?" Carla asked.

"Sure did, called a place over in Quincy, they got a nice one ready for tomorrow morning. Got it for the whole day."

He'd asked for an inboard, V-hull boat, not a johnboat like he'd had when he was a teenager. Although johnboats were good if you hugged the banks, out in the channel they were almost impossible to control in the high waves, especially if a barge passed by, raising a huge wake.

CHAPTER 18

CORNELIUS BONOMONO

My job at the docks was pretty boring because I was there to make sure nothing got out of hand from the mob's perspective, and it never seemed to get out of hand. The fact that nothing happened was actually what I was supposed to do. Mostly I just hung around the offices and read some books and did crossword puzzles or played on the computer.

The docks are actually run by both the Italian and Irish mobs, kind of a division down the middle and it's been this way for maybe eighty or ninety years, so it's got a long, long tradition. I was on the Italian side of the fence, but since I always hung around with Irish guys before, I got to know more of them from the docks. Little by little my role changed and both sides got to trusting me and I became what you might call a go-between in the two groups. Not that they had a lot of conflicts, but from time to time conflicts came up, it's only natural because the Irish and the Italians had so many things they did different. It's two different cultures, really. The Italians, they stick together closer than the Irish do, but the Irish are cagey, creative and can be mean when they need to be. Both sides kept one eye on the other.

Pretty soon Sonny Ianetta came to me and asked me if I would want to approach the head of the Irish mob with a request he had for a new way of working the harbor. The plan was to move harder in the direction of taking over some of the new technology that was coming into fashion by the people who owned the ships. I said yes I'd do that and I made overtures to meet with Brian Mahoney, the head of the Irish mob. He seemed to be a real nice guy but I knew he had a reputation for being ruthless and him and I sort of hit it off and I explained what Sonny wanted to do. The long and short of it was that I was the go-between on this whole new deal, and both sides came to trust me.

I ended up doing a lot more of going between the two sides in the next two years and pretty soon I'm getting a reputation as a problem-solver, somebody who both sides like and trust. It's a hard position to maintain because you got to be honest and truthful, and make sure messages are relayed in a correct way. You also have to be courteous, never step outside your boundaries, and respectful. The more I got to do this stuff the more I realized that both sides actually had lots of stuff in common, but there were always guys on either side who wanted to stir things up. My old friend Jimmy Olivetti was one of them, he'd gotten to be a hothead and Sonny had to pull him in a few times and tell him to cool it. Also, Jimmy Cochran was rising with the Irish gang and he wasn't a troublemaker, but still as looney as could be, and always coming up with these big ideas about how to score more money and he liked to rock the boat. He I liked, but Jimmy Olivetti I grew to not like. Something had changed in him, he just got meaner with age.

My big test came because of Jimmy Olivetti. He had beaten the shit out of one of the Irish guys over nothing at all, just one of those barroom conversations that gets out of hand. I was pulled in for about six different meetings where the Irish and the Italians were head to head over it. Fortunately cooler heads prevailed. I didn't play a huge role in it, but I did say that this had to be settled if everyone was going to get along and make some money at the docks. Everyone shook their head in agreement after I said that and it was settled. I think my stock went up with both sides because of that incident.

The two bosses came to an agreement about me. I was to be paid by both sides, in equal amounts, and I was to be the go-between that started negotiations to settle any conflicts or disagreements. I wasn't a judge really, the decisions would stay with the bosses, but I was the common ground, maybe like the United Nations or Switzerland. It was a job I really enjoyed and I think I was pretty good at it.

CHAPTER 19

BARNEY COMPONARI

I've known Jack now only five years but it's like we've known each other all of our lives. I've been an expert witness for a lot of attorneys and mostly I don't like them but Jack is different. First off, he has no pretensions, and when someone at his firm told me he cut his own hair I believed it right away. A guy who cuts his own hair when he has enough money to go to the best hair salon in Boston is someone I wanted to know more. Sometimes we'd sit in his office and laugh our assess off at some of the stuff he and I were working on, and I think if the clients knew what we were saying about them – both his clients and my patients – they would have fired us on the spot.

I had sort of an epiphany one day, maybe a revelation even, like it came over me and I had a clarity I'd never had before. It was a peaceful feeling like everything would be okay. When I was a kid sometimes I'd get a feeling like that and it was hard to describe but I hadn't had a feeling like that since I was a kid.

When I did my training at Harvard there were some old guys in the business who even still used terms like insane asylums and crazy, and these guys were psychiatrists. I thought they were Neanderthals and gave them wide berth. The more I was around them though the more I came to appreciate their experience, sometimes their insights into mental illnesses, even their cynical senses of humor. They had seen a lot more than me and they had all sorts of different theories about why people acted the way they did. They had been trained in the days before all the technology and the new generations of psycho-active drugs, so they had to rely on insights and gut instincts.

When I started my own practice it never ceased to amaze me the behavior that can come from the human species. Nothing could surprise me, nothing could shock me. Sometimes a psychiatrist has to resist taking on some of the thoughts and even symptoms of his patients because you're around crazy people all the time. See, I used it, too, the word crazy, just like those old guys in the business years ago.

As I got older and my practice even more established I thought back about those old guys and thought maybe I was getting like them. It wasn't burnout, really, but just struggling with trying to come up with some theory that held everything together. Maybe physicists or astronomers reach that point too where they know so much but then they realize they don't know anything at all, that the universe is a very mysterious place that doesn't give up its secrets easily.

One night I was at home and bored with television and found a book on the table that my daughter had brought home over the Christmas holidays and left at home. It was the Divine Comedy and I was bored so I opened it, sat down in a chair, and started reading it. Of course I'd heard about it and even looked up on Wikipedia a description of the book. At first I thought it was hard to read and I put it down after about fifteen minutes. The next night I picked it up again, and then again, and then again. In about two weeks' time I couldn't wait to get back to it. My wife was puzzled why I stayed up so late in bed with the light on, carefully reading it. It was kind of like climbing a mountain because it doesn't reveal itself right away and you have to work at it to understand all of its meanings and I didn't even think I was getting all of its deeper meanings. I was absolutely amazed that one man had written the whole thing, how the hell did he have those insights and wisdom? And I found out that he'd been a pretty young guy when he wrote it.

That was the reason for my epiphany I think. It started me down the road to thinking about things differently, that things were choreographed by God, that there were consequences to actions, that there was good and evil, and free will and an order to the universe that was just beyond our limited vision.

I don't think Jack understands why I've turned much more philosophical. Sometimes he looks at me like I'm speaking gibberish because I'll use terms like evil, or crazy or that they belong in an insane asylum. Just like those old guys I worked with years ago. I look at some of the medical students in a class I still teach at Harvard, full of theories and knowledge about new technology in pharmacology and I wonder if some of them think of me like I did of the old guys, way behind the times. Well, maybe one day when they're older they may remember me and say hey that guy had a point.

CHAPTER 20

LUCY WETTERAU

A gorgeous day to be on the river. About 80 degrees, huge fluffy clouds high in the sky, sun bright as could be, wind not too strong. Jack edged the boat out from its moorings at Quincy harbor and headed out to the main channel, opened it up and headed north. In about half an hour he spotted Hogback Island, about a dozen boats floating just off the sandy beach. He could hear the music already, almost smell the beer.

"I think we can avoid that place, it's mostly drunk kids, they get louder and drunker as the day goes on. Spent many an afternoon there. Let's go farther north."

"You're in command. Take me where you will," Carla said, wearing a one-piece bathing suit that was, as Jack expected it to be, cute. She really had a very attractive figure, he thought.

They cruised past Canton, on the Missouri side. "I had a lot of friends over there. We'd meet up north on the river on weekends, tie our boats together and make it one big party."

He slowed the boat, running close to the Missouri side, taking in the shoreline, watching for submerged logs up ahead. As they glided past the shoreline, he told Carla about he and Lucy finding the body up in this part of the river.

"You want to go to where we found that body?"

"Sure."

He throttled up the boat, crossed the river at an angle, medium speed.

He wasn't so sure he was right where he needed to be, sloughs can change over the years, cut new courses. He entered one, cruised along at a very slow speed because he wasn't so sure of the depth, and this boat drew a much bigger draught that a johnboat.

"We'll have to go real slow because I don't know how deep it is, or what kind of shit could be below."

Just as he said this he heard a light scraping on the hull. He stopped the boat, let it slide aside a bit. Apparently what it had hit had passed.

"Hope that's not another body, Jack."

"No such luck. Lightning never strikes twice in the same place."

He decided to back out of the slough. "I think it's just too shallow. This could be the right one, but this boat's a little too big to come in these sloughs."

"Let's get back in the river, it's too hot back here anyway," she said.

They got back in the channel just as a barge was heading south. Barges on the Mississippi are huge, stretching sometimes four city blocks, pushed by towboats that are just gigantic diesel engines with a few rooms attached for a conning tower and mess hall for deckhands. Close to 400 million tons of goods move up and down the Mississippi every year, in towboats with twin propellers of four blades each as tall as a man, powered by 5,000-horsepower engines. You never want to be near a towboat as it passes, their wakes too strong and turbulent.

Near sunset they docked the boat, went into Quincy for dinner.

"I had an absolutely great time," Carla said. "I've lived near this river now for two years but only once was I in it, and that was just a friend's little sailboat. Being out in the middle I had no idea how big it is. It's actually kind of scary."

"I never took this river for granted. I shudder to think the risks we took on it when we were teenagers. We didn't even wear lifejackets, thought that was too uncool. We actually even waterskied back in those sloughs, with all that crap just below the surface. You're invincible when you're young."

The drive from Quincy to Carthage goes through some of the prettiest land Jack could imagine, gently rolling slopes opening up to dead-flat fields of corn and soybeans. Then, another set of small hills. You have to make sure you stay awake, don't nod off because the drive can be so hypnotic, especially when it's dark.

Because of that it's always good to have someone in the car with you, although Carla had fallen asleep. Even her soft snoring was cute.

Her cell phone clanged, startling both of them. They were ten minutes from Carthage. Carla looked at the number, took the call.

"Yeah, Brett, what's going on?"

Jack only heard Carla's side of the conversation.

"Uh huh...uh huh...yes, I got it, thanks Brett. We'll be right over."

"What was that about?" Jack asked.

"That was one of the sheriff's deputies," she said. "Lucy killed herself."

Jack was stunned, slowed down on the highway to digest the news.

"How did she do it?"

"She tore a metal towel rack off the wall in the shower, jammed it right through her neck. The guards were there but it happened so fast nobody could have done a thing."

They arrived at the county hospital, a couple of cop cars parked outside the emergency room.

"She's in that room," a nurse said, pointing to a small cubicle with curtain drawn. "You relatives?"

"We're her attorneys...I mean, we were her attorneys," Carla said.

She was covered in a sheet, head to toe. They pulled it back, Lucy's face flaccid, gray, drained. A huge, jagged wound clearly illustrated the raw violence of her action.

The two stood there silent.

CHAPTER 21

LARRY MAGUIRE

Things just spun out of control one day when I went to see Jimmy Tracadora. We met for a few minutes at his office, if you could describe it as such, and then he asked me if I'd like to go along with him to another meeting he had downtown. He said he had to meet with a guy connected with the organization somehow and was someone I should meet. I could figure out that Jimmy wasn't asking me if I wanted to go, that he was telling me to go.

I got in Jimmy's car and we started out, but it was obvious that it wasn't downtown where we were going. Instead, he headed south and I asked him this wasn't the way downtown but he said well this guy doesn't actually work downtown, but on the south side, and Jimmy won't look at me while he's talking and that's starting to make me very nervous, my bowels were getting all squishy and I thought I'd take a shit right in my pants. We stopped at an old building and Jimmy got out of the car and I got out too and he says he has to go inside and see this guy but I could stay in the car until he came out the door and waved me inside.

I thought well this might be where they kill me, and I'm thinking about running away but then I know there's nowhere to go and if I run then they know I'm about ready to be killed. I can't even think straight and I'm starting to panic but then Jimmy comes out the door and waves me to come in the door. My legs were so wobbly it must have shown because I almost staggered to the door. Jimmy is smiling and he tells me to follow him and I go and the building is kind of dark and we go down a narrow hallway, him about four or five feet ahead of me. We walk through a door and it opens up into a big room, like an old warehouse. He turns on a light and the room is empty, except for something in a corner. He walks over to a corner and there's a guy sitting in a chair, only he's not just sitting, he's slumped over and tied to the chair. His face is all bloody and swollen and he's just barely moving and moaning a little bit.

Jimmy and I are looking at the guy and without saying a word Jimmy walks up right next to the guy and pulls a gun out and shoots the guy in the head. It's not like in the movies, with blood everywhere. It just goes in one side and that's it, just a small hole in the side of the head. Then he shoots him again right in the head and then puts the gun back in his pocket. Then Jimmy turns to me and he just has this weird look on his face and says this is what happens to guys who are disloyal. That's all he said, then he said let's get out of this place, and we got back in the car and Jimmy delivered me back to his office and I got in my car and drove away. We didn't say a word to each other the whole ride.

CHAPTER 22

CARLA COLLINS PORTER

"You think there was anything to that story about her boyfriend?" Carla asked as they ate breakfast at a diner across from the courthouse the next morning after Lucy's suicide. "Or you think that was just her raving."

"I truly don't know, how could I know? He's dead, she's dead, how would anyone know? It could be a bunch of bullshit or just the tip of the iceberg of a worldwide child porn syndicate. No way to know."

"I think she was telling the truth. I think she committed suicide when she came to her senses, realized what she had done, or what she had become. She just wanted a way out," Carla said.

"You could be right," he said.

"You going to tell the sheriff what she told us?" Jack asked.

"Sure. It's a possible lead in a case, I think we'd be remiss not to mention it. Maybe someone else over in Hamilton knows more about this story. Maybe those guys she mentioned, the bees."

Jack went to the funeral home, talked with them about what would happen to Lucy's body, what about her funeral. Nothing, really, they told her, she'd just be cremated. Jack asked to see the casket selection, chose one that looked nice, and asked what it would cost for a service and burial. He charged it on his American Express card.

He left Carthage after leaving the funeral home, headed to Chicago's Midway Airport. He'd booked himself on an earlier flight, would get back to Boston earlier, time to settle in before a busy week. It would probably be a long time before he saw Carthage again. No reason to.

Jack usually worked while on a flight, but this time he just gazed out the window, looking down at the ground below, thinking about what had just occurred in Hancock County, why Lucy had spiraled downward so far, ended up as she did, drugged out with shit-bums like Eddie Crane. Obviously her life had gotten so desperate that she felt the compulsion to drive a piece of metal straight through her neck.

Jack and his partners were familiar with people committing suicide, having had a half dozen clients do so during the years. Again, Barney had given him some insights into the whys of suicide. He said people don't just decide to commit suicide in the spur of the moment. It's not like they're walking across a bridge and say to themselves 'this is a good time to die' and leap to their death. Although they may do it without warning to others, they've been thinking about it for a long time, maybe years. One day they decide this is the day and they jump, or pull the trigger. It looks spur-of-the-moment, but it's not. A lot of the rules of what we think of as normal go out the window when you talk about suicide.

Back in his condominium he hurried to bed, exhausted by the weekend. He couldn't help but keep thinking about Lucy and what she had done. How does a person's life spiral downward like that?

The next day he did a Google search on Carla Collins Porter. Graduate of Mount Holyoke College in Massachusetts as she'd mentioned. Her ex-husband Peter was an architect. He found a photograph of her from an awards ceremony at Chicago Kent Law School.

"Carla Collins Porter, left, receives an award from the school for her generous contribution of $10 million to be used to set up a program to assist free legal clinics throughout Illinois," the photo's cutline read.

 Collins Porter…of course. How oblivious could he be? Collins Porter was a man's name, a turn-of-the-century Chicago industrialist who made a fortune in both steel and lumber. No wonder the artwork, the desk. That wasn't the property of Hancock County.

He phoned her.

"I think my great grandfather worked for your great-grandfather."

"A lot of people worked for my great-grandfather."

"I should have had you pay for the boat and the dinners."

She laughed.

"Is that Winslow Homer the original?"

"No, the original is in Paris. But I own it."

"Jack, don't be a stranger. The river's always here. I'll pay my share of the boat next time. Dinner too. As much spaghetti as you want."

CHAPTER 23

BRIAN MCINTOSH

After he arrived back to Boston from Carthage Jack had probably the biggest setback of his career. He was censured by the Massachusetts Bar for what it characterized as behavior not in line with "commonly held ethical practices." It was fancy bar association language for lying. The Boston Globe published a small item on the back page. He'd never been in the news before except for puff pieces on cases he'd won, or how successful his firm had become. It was a shock to get negative publicity.

"Don't get your undies in a bundle," Maguire said, "this shit happens all the time. Wait a year, make an appeal, and they'll rescind the ruling."

The ruling had come about as a complaint from a former client who claimed Jack had doctored documents to cover his tracks that would have showed malfeasance and incompetence. The defendant, a financial executive accused by a co-worker of rape, had claimed that he doctored the documents to hide the fact that he'd been late in filing appeals that would have resulted in an exoneration of the client.

It was all bullshit, the executive having been accused by several women in the past of sexual assaults but never charged before. He was guilty but trying to salvage what was left of his shabby reputation by blaming his attorney. It happened from time to time, but Jack had never been the victim of such a charge. There were two members of the board of directors of the bar association who hated Jack and no doubt advocated for the charge based upon little or no evidence. It was payback. Regardless, as Jack so well understood, the accusation is as bad as the conviction in the eyes of the public.

He phoned Brian McIntosh, who ran a public relations firm. He'd met McIntosh years ago when he'd first arrived in Boston, both of them poor guys hanging around the bars in Chelsea. Like Jack, McIntosh had made it good, a bottom-feeder who now was successful. In fact, it was McIntosh who had introduced Jack to his first wife, Barbara.

"Got time for lunch, Brian? I've got a public relations matter to discuss. Consider it just as if you had a legal problem. I'd charge you, so you charge me, okay?"

"You think I would do this for free? With the amount of money you make chiseling all those people?

"How about tomorrow, Legal Sea Foods, downtown, noon?" McIntosh asked.

"See you there."

The next day the two sat in a back booth. Legal Sea Foods was McIntosh's favorite place, he said he'd eat there every day if he could. A red-faced Irish Catholic, he was Boston through and through, a no bullshit guy, funny as hell.

"I saw the story, Jack," Brian said. "I got some quick advice for you and listen to me very closely. You'd better get out of town, and stay away for several years until this blows over."

For a second he didn't realize McIntosh was joking.

"Just kidding you, don't look so glum, bud," McIntosh said.

"Cool your jets. When people get their asses in a sling publically they think the world's crashing in on them. Back away from it if you can and think about all the things you hear about that you don't give one shit about. Well, everybody's got their own problems, they don't care about you being in the paper just this once."

McIntosh said in most cases unfavorable stories have just the opposite effect, unless the story is of a horrible nature, or if the negative stories keep coming. Most of the time bad publicity is still publicity, and in many cases actually helps because it improves a person's name recognition.

"Unless you hurt either a kid or a dog most people are very understanding, and forgiving," he said.

"Here's what to do. Don't say anything, just like you tell your clients. Don't write a press release, don't go to the papers, if anyone from the press calls, just avoid them. If you say anything it just gives those pricks at the bar a next-day story, something that keeps the story alive. The headline is 'Jack LaPoint fights ethics charge.' Nobody remember the 'fights' part, just the 'ethics charge' part."

"Cool it. It will go away. If they come at you again, then it's another situation. Then you need to counterpunch and I can help you do that. But my inclination is this is just a single rabbit-punch."

"What do I owe you for your advice?" Jack asked.

"The $22.99 halibut special, with hush puppies."

As usual, McIntosh's instincts were correct. The accusation was buried, went away. The publicity didn't seem to bring in any new business, but it didn't hurt the firm either.

Later that week wasn't any better. Sarah phoned.

"You got time to meet?" She asked. He knew immediately it wasn't for fun and games.

"I can tell from your voice you have something to tell me."

"I do, Jack, but not over the phone."

At lunch, the two sat at a small café in the Back Bay.

"I met someone at the hospital, Jack. He's a doctor in the oncology center. I think it's getting serious. He wants me to move in with him."

Jack didn't answer right away. As many times as he's been rejected by women in his life, it didn't get any easier. He looked at Sarah, she had her head down, avoided his eyes.

"When did you start seeing him Sarah? Not that it matters, just that I'm curious."

"Three or four months ago. He asked me out, and I went out to dinner with him. We've been seeing each other pretty much every week."

"Is he married, Sarah?"

"No, a widower."

"Is he your age?"

"No, he's a little bit older. Getting ready to retire, actually."

"What's his name?"

"David Fairfield."

"Sarah, you and I have good times together. I really enjoy your company, but I guess if I had met someone else we might be at this same table talking about the same thing, only in reverse."

He could see some of the weight lift from her shoulders. She looked at him.

"Let's have lunch, Sarah, enjoy ourselves. I hope he's right for you. You deserve it," Jack said.

She was crying. "I'm so sorry, Jack."

It hurt, but not as much as when Lucy told him 30 years ago she was going out with Steve Andros. What was it about him that made other women fall in love with someone else?

As if that wasn't enough bad news, his week got worse when he read in the Globe that the body of Bradford Spellman had been found down by the Charles River. It was a big story, front page, and went into details of the trial at which Jack had been able to secure a not guilty verdict for Spellman in the murder-for-hire case of his partner. Police were quoted as saying it appeared to be an execution-style killing, two shots to the head with a .22 caliber weapon. There were marks on the body that indicated he had been tortured and bound.

CHAPTER 24

CARLA COLLINS PORTER

This sounds weird to say, but it was never my fault that I was born into a wealthy family. It's not something you can say to anyone because it sounds so inappropriate. Everybody would think "Well, isn't that a shame, too much money."

Everybody thinks that if you have lots of money that somehow your life is different from what everyone else experiences. In a few ways it is, because you have access to a lot of things. But having access to lots of things doesn't mean you don't suffer from the same things that everyone else does.

In my case the thing that I had to put up with was being alone, and being lonely. I was separate from a lot of the kids at school, separate from a lot of people because we had so much money. I would lay awake some nights when I was a kid and wish that I could be more like them, wear clothes that weren't new, have parents who drove old cars, went to regular grocery stores and didn't have maids and other people around to do our work.

I liked my dad a lot more than my mom. Of course I never said that to anyone, but when my dad would come home from work my day brightened. He was always so nice and glad to see me. Sometimes he'd have candy in his pocket for me and my brother, he'd spend time with us asking about what we did that day, what he'd done or seen.

My mother was not that friendly, even cold you could say. She was beautiful, always carefully dressed and with the best clothes. Later when I had a better vocabulary I thought of her as imperial.

Kathy Ludig was probably my best friend. She was from a rich family, too, and her parents were divorced, and neither her dad nor mom was very nice to her and her sister Liz. Both of them were pretty much raised by nannies. Liz eventually became a heroin addict and had to be sent up to a fancy rehab center in Minnesota. Kathy married a guy who I hated and I knew he was just after her money, but Kathy was head over heels about him. It lasted a couple of years, then he got caught screwing a neighbor, so that was the end of him.

Because I didn't have a lot of friends I spent a lot of time reading and day-dreaming about stuff. I day-dreamed about the kind of guy I might meet and eventually marry. You could say I was a romantic that way, although not many guys asked me out in high school, or even in college. I guess I wasn't sexy or voluptuous enough, more like the friendly girl who was in the background. I went to Mount Holyoke College in Massachusetts, which was a big change for me because I grew up in the Midwest. I met all sorts of girls from all over the country, and my best friend Beth came from a small town in Kansas, where her dad was a car dealer. We did a lot together during college, even spent a semester in Spain, which I loved.

Beth and I graduated together and she went on to medical school and did so well, getting a residency at Johns Hopkins, and then going into private practice in New York City, where she has an office right on Park Avenue. She made gobs of money, and every once in a while I'd see her and we'd go to lunch and laugh so hard we'd almost wet our pants.

I met Peter in Chicago. He was just starting at an architecture firm, and didn't have a lot of money but that certainly didn't bother me. He was tall, dark-haired, lots of fun, wooed me like no man had before. He was the first guy with whom I had real sex. He swept me off my feet.

We had two sons, and lived outside of Chicago in a big house up in Kenilworth. I mostly volunteered and stayed home raising the two boys. It was fun up there, making friends with other women who were in the same boat. Through all that time I still read constantly, and day-dreamed, too.

One of my best friends was also my next-door neighbor, which is really special. Deb Adamian was from the south side of Chicago, her dad a Chicago policeman, her mother a teacher. She and I would drink some wine in the afternoons before the kids got home from school, and we'd sit around and laugh and gossip. Her husband was a big-time finance guy down on LaSalle Street, and she always complained that he was never home, always preoccupied with some big deal he was concocting.

Deb's afternoon drinking began to extend further and further into the evenings, and I started to get concerned when she'd start drinking hours before I got to the house in the afternoon. She slurred her words every once in a while and I could tell that she was unhappy with her situation at home.

She must have hit bottom because they put her into a rehab center and she came home dried out, but somehow changed in a big way. She wasn't as free and easy as she had been, much more subdued. Then one day I saw an ambulance at her house. She had tried to commit suicide, but one of her kids found her up in bed and right away called 911 when they had trouble getting her awake.

Back she went to a place in Wisconsin this time, and she entered some sort of program where she went through therapy and then went to some sort of half-way house in Milwaukee. I went up there a lot to see her and she seemed very happy there. She told me she'd met a man there and had fallen in love. She begged me to keep it a secret, which I did. The guy was a carpenter who she met while he was doing some work at the halfway house. "He's a dreamboat," she told me, like it was some teenage romance from the 1950s.

She filed for divorce, got a little money from the settlement, and married the carpenter. They moved up to Rhinelander, Wisconsin, up in the boonies and started a small construction company. I kept in touch with her from time to time and she had found her place in the world. We drifted apart and she eventually became just another name on the Christmas card list.

My marriage to Peter wasn't going so well, and I couldn't figure if it was just that time in life when married couples transform into roommates or if there was something seriously wrong. Peter's architecture career had taken off and he spent more and more time downtown. I never suspected he had any other woman in his life, never crossed my mind. Then, out of the blue, he tells me that he wants to get an apartment downtown, someplace he can stay when he has to stay at work late and doesn't want to take the train home. I thought it kind of strange, but he said we both could stay there. I didn't know it at the time but he'd already gotten an apartment about a month earlier.

I asked him if he had a girlfriend and he said no. I believed him. Stupid me. A friend of mine called one day and asked if I had time for lunch. I thought she needed help about something, but it turned out she had agonized about whether or not to tell me that Peter was seeing a graduate student at the University of Chicago.

It took my breath away, I got dizzy when she told me the world started spinning, literally. I think I halfway fell out of my chair, my friend getting up to help me straighten myself. My friend tried to hold me, but I wrenched away, the glass of wine I'd been drinking flung across the room.

For the rest of that day and well into the night I sat in my bedroom, not moving, just looking out the window into our back yard. I wasn't really thinking about anything, more catatonic than conscious.

I called Peter about midnight. "I heard about your affair, Peter," I told him.

He didn't say anything at first, and I didn't either.

Finally he said. "I'm sorry, Carla. I was going to tell you."

I hung up without saying a word. The next morning I called my lawyer, and that was it.

For the following year I was a lost soul, roaming around the house, feeling so sorry for myself. I didn't go out, didn't see many friends. I lost weight and looked like hell. I took a couple of trips down to Florida to see my brother, but when I came home I'd just sit around and mope. I was depressed, but felt entitled to it, that I'd earned it.

A friend suggested that I go to graduate school; that I was still young enough to carve out a career for myself. I mulled that over for a few months but couldn't figure out what I'd like to do. One of my brother's friends, an attorney, asked if I'd like to meet for lunch. He was recently divorced and I think this was a date. We met downtown and had a great time, although I wasn't interested in him in any romantic way. He just wasn't my type, if there ever was a "my type."

But he got me thinking about going to law school. I did my homework, asked around to where I might be able to get in, how to take the LSATs and what I might be able to do with a law degree.

I got into law school and I loved it, unlike a lot of my classmates. I was much older than most of them, probably a lot more motivated, too. The logic of the law fascinated me; sometimes I was so interested that I didn't even have to take notes. Even the classes that everybody thought were boring, like contracts, I loved.

I passed the bar on the first try, and started to look for jobs. I interviewed at a lot of law firms, and I think the fact that I was wealthy was actually a disadvantage. They assumed that I would never be hungry enough to work hard, that I'd just quit when the going got tough. I didn't think so; I was so excited about being a lawyer.

I found out about the public defenders' jobs all across the state. Many of the more rural counties had a very difficult time filling those jobs, which didn't pay much and actually weren't considered very prestigious. I didn't care.

There were a dozen counties that were salivating for anyone to take the public defender's position. I literally put a map of Illinois down on the floor and threw three coins on it. The first one to land on one of those dozen counties would be where I'd apply. The second coin landed squarely in the middle of Hancock County. I'd never even heard of the place but I could see it was just along the Mississippi River.

I applied and got the job. I closed up the house, the boys were just getting ready to go to college and I packed my bags and went to Carthage. I loved it immediately, the folks at the courthouse so welcoming. It really didn't matter to me, I was just so eager to start my first case. A guy named Elwood Manchester walked in, actually walked in using a walker, and he told me the bank had foreclosed on his farm and he had no money to hire an attorney to make his case to both the county and the bank. He was my first client. Then, a woman named Aratha Symington walked in later that week and her daughter had been charged with selling crack cocaine over in Hamilton, and she needed an attorney. I was off and running.

I was really happy. Carthage seemed like it had always been my home. At first I lived out of motel, then I found a place right downtown, an old building that had once been a hardware store. I had it redone into a condominium.

CHAPTER 25

BRIAN MCINTOSH

Oh, I've known Jack for years and he's just one of those guys who you want to hang out with, although neither of us have much time for doing that anymore. He's the guy who goes to a really fine Italian restaurant and orders spaghetti. He did that once at this fancy-ass restaurant when my girlfriend and I met him and another gal about a year ago on the North End. When the waiter said we don't serve spaghetti here sir, you have to go down to the Tivoli for that, I nearly spat my water out on the table. The Tivoli is a dive that's been in the North End for centuries and the joke is that you never see any stray dogs or cats near that restaurant.

I never had a plan in my life, only that I wanted to make some money and have some fun. In school I never had anything that really interested me, and I was one of those C students always in the picture, hanging out with friends and having a good time. I lived for the parties on weekends.

They say the Irish are good at two things – drinking and talking. Well, I fit into that stereotype perfectly. Talk was the coin of the realm in my family, we talked all the time, every one of us. When I met my first wife I remember going over to her house for Sunday night dinner and they hardly talked at all. I couldn't believe it and it made me feel so uncomfortable that I jiggled around in my chair at the dinner table, all nervous. I tried to bring up subject after subject and I'd get a polite nod but not much more than that. I thought maybe they were just being quiet to check me out, but the next time I went there it was the same deal. How in the hell could people sit around, people who grew up together even, and not talk?

There must be something way far back when the Irish were huddled around fires in the cold and dark when they told stories to each other to distract themselves from how miserable their lives were. That I figured was the dawn of bullshit and it set roots deep in their DNA. Bullshit was a way to get through the day, or the night. I didn't have much going for me when I was young but I sure knew how to talk with people, and I couldn't remember a time when it wasn't that way.

I told my wife when she wasn't yet my wife that eating dinner over at her parents' house was torture for me. So I said why don't we have one dinner with my parents sometime? My parents were so excited that I even had a girlfriend that they wouldn't shut up at dinner. She told me on the way home she didn't know people could talk non-stop about really nothing at all.

The first time I ran into Jack LaPoint was at the Lion's Den over in Chelsea. I remember it was a beautiful summer day because I remember thinking I should be outside on a day like that and not in a dark bar having a beer. Jack was the only other person at the bar and we got to talking. To tell you the truth I didn't think he was all that impressive, but I think I did all the talking. It was all the kind of stupid-shit bar talk, the Red Sox and Patriots. It was probably a ten-minute conversation and he told me he had to get back to work and left. I saw him there a couple of times and we kind of formed a bar friendship of sorts, we were both the same age and kind of sick of our jobs. He worked at a law firm downtown and I was working at a little PR firm near Copley Square. He told me where he was from but I kept forgetting, Indiana or Ohio or one of those states.

We got to hanging out together and he even introduced me to guys who lived next door to him and who he hung out with from time to time. They were two goombas and I didn't think they were guys he should be hanging out with and I told him that, too, but he said they were okay. Fine with me but I wasn't going to hang out with those guys.

I got let go at my agency because they lost their biggest client and they let go of a bunch of us all on the same day. There was a local politician by the name of Larry Riceberg and I knew a guy who worked for him. I got in to see Riceberg and convinced him he needed a guy to gin up some positive publicity for him. He said he wasn't going to pay me until I got him some good press. I said if I got him one story in the Globe that he'd owe me $2,000. We had a deal. I hustled my ass off and in a month I got him a short puff piece in the Globe and he paid me on the day it appeared. Then I got him a piece in the Herald and I got $1,500.

I didn't even have an office and I never realized I was starting a PR company until it was up and running. It fit me like a glove and two more politicians hired me to make them look good. Then a guy who had a big dog food company hired me and I made the dog food company look good. I was still hanging around with Jack and he told me that he was thinking about going out on his own too. Then he got fired from his job and he said he had to go it alone for sure. We kind of lost touch after that because I got so busy and he did, too, but we'd bump into each other every once in a while although we'd traded up from the Lion's Den in Chelsea to a bunch of better class bars downtown. We stayed good friends because we were both "I-knew-you-back-when" buddies.

CHAPTER 26

SARAH COLLINGSWORTH

A lot of people call it the city of the sick and dying, the huge complex of hospitals in downtown Boston. There's actually four big hospitals all smashed together and I worked at just one of them, the children's hospital.

Sometimes during my lunch break I would go down to the huge cafeteria just to get away from the stuff going on at the ICU. You can go kind of zombie-like down there and a lot of people would sit by themselves, staff people like me or family members there because someone's sick.

One day this guy came up to me at my table and asked if I minded if he sat down there. Sure, I said and I recognized him but didn't know who he was. It turned out he was an oncologist over at Mass Gen. We had a nice little visit and then went on our ways. About a week later I saw him in the cafeteria and went up to him and asked if he wanted company. He had a great smile and I thought it was cute that he brought his own lunch in a brown paper bag. He asked me out right then and there and I said yes. It just seemed so natural.

I didn't think it would be a big problem with Jack because we had a sort of an agreement. We were like buddies who slept together from time to time. It wasn't that casual, we cared about one another but it was somewhere between platonic and a love affair, it's really hard to explain.

Just to be on the safe side I chose a place in a neighborhood that I knew Jack would never visit. I had David, that's his name, David, pick me up at my house and we had a great time just talking the night away. It seemed that I poured out my life to him and he listened. He told me about his life, too, that he had three grown kids who he adored and how his wife died and what he thought about his oncology practice. He was 63 years old, just 10 years older than me, and he was thinking about hanging it up and doing something completely different like helping out his brother-in-law down in Chatham who had a fishing fleet. Both he and I loved the ocean it turned out.

I was head over heels crazy about this guy and it's like my life changed around completely. My kids had no idea what had come over me and my daughter kept pressing me about what was going on in my life. I told her about David and I remember her just putting her hand over her mouth and saying Oh Mom so that's what it's all about. I thought that if David was thinking seriously about running off to a fishing fleet on the Cape I wanted to be right there with him.

CHAPTER 27

HOWARD BOWLAND, MD

Jack had always had a rocky relationship with the medical profession. He occasionally took on malpractice cases, although they weren't his favorite. He couldn't count any doctors among his close friends, and he hated going to the doctor himself. He was convinced that if he went he'd find out he was dying of some horrible ailment. A lot of men were like that.

He forced himself to see his doctor once a year, trudging in to see Howard Bowland as if he was going to the gallows.

"Jack, good to see you again," Bowland said as he walked into the examination room.

"Good to see you again, doctor," Jack answered.

The ritual began. Bowland sat down on a swivel stool, looked at Jack and said "How you feeling?"

"Pretty good. No big problems."

"Good, good. Let me take a look at you," he said, pulling out the blood pressure cuff from a drawer nearby. He wrapped the cuff around Jack's arm, listened carefully for a few seconds. "Hmmm, a little high, but not too bad."

"You been exercising, Jack?"

"No."

"How's your diet?"

"Shitty."

"You feeling any chest pains, acid reflux, having trouble sleeping, that sort of thing?"

"No, nothing."

"You peeing and pooping alright?"

"Yes."

"What about depression? Any of that?"

"No."

"Let's take a look." He listened to his heart, had Jack lay down on the examination table, probed his abdomen area, checked his glands around his neck, looked at his ears, throat, eyes.

"What are you looking for in all these things you do?" Jack asked.

"Nothing, just have to justify my fee. Basically I don't know what the hell I'm doing," Bowland said, deadpan. Then he laughed. "Just kidding. No, I'm looking for any unusual bumbs, lumps, sounds that don't sound right, things that look suspicious. You know, despite all the technology we have today this sort of exam is essential, nothing can replace the old basics. If I find something that raises any alarms, then I throw you at the machines."

"Got to tell you, though, Jack, your blood work looks a little out of whack. Your blood sugar is higher than I like to see, your cholesterol is getting above what's normal. You're showing your age, and your lifestyle."

"There's only one answer for you, Jack. If you want to get everything back to normal, you have to exercise. Join a gym, get to the Y, anything. I'll tell you that I had almost the same numbers myself a couple of years ago, and three or four workouts a week got them right back to normal. Check it out."

Bowland continued. "Of course none of my patients take my advice. I say this stuff all day to men and women just like you and hardly anyone follows my advice. It's like your own profession probably. How many of your clients actually follow your advice? You talk till you're blue in the face, they nod their heads in agreement, walk out of your office and go do whatever the hell they want to do."

"Oh, you got that right. Where is your gym?" Jack asked.

"I just use the Y downtown, it's much cheaper. Don't buy equipment and say you're going to exercise at home because you won't. You have to go somewhere and exercise, you'll be forced to do it if you show up somewhere," Bowland said.

The next day he entered the YMCA downtown, taking the walk of shame into the locker room. After 15 minutes on the exercise bike he was exhausted. Fortunately there were plenty of men there who looked much the same. Maybe he'd start coming every other morning.

Weekends were pretty lonely without Sarah, but he still went to Lake Sunapee. He began hiking, thinking that may help him get in shape. He actually appreciated some of the time alone.

His cell phone rang one Saturday night, fairly late, about 9 p.m. as he was getting ready for bed.

"It's Carla, Jack. I have some news. Lucy definitely didn't kill Eddie Crane. They found another guy murdered over in Hamilton. His throat was cut. His home had all sorts of film equipment, he was our child porn guy. Looks like Lucy wasn't telling any tales, Eddie had to be working for this guy."

"Who's the dead guy?"

"Man named Sherry Garand. He's got a woman's name."

"Any clues?"

"Sheriff told me nothing of any substance, but I think it's because they don't have much. The guy wasn't quite the loser Eddie was. Had some money, lived in a pretty nice house, had a respectable job with one of the companies over there. Lived alone."

They talked about the case for a few minutes.

"Change of subject, how have you been, Carla?"

"Very well, boys are here this weekend, we're having fun."

"You up for another spin on the river?" Jack asked.

"Yup. Love to, but we better do it soon, it's starting to get cool in the evenings around here."

"How about this weekend? I can get there Friday night, check into the Days Inn, we can be ready to go the next day. I'll stay through Monday, learn a little bit more about what went on in Hamilton. If you wouldn't mind I'd like to do a little fishing on the river. You don't mind, do you?"

"I'm not the fishing type, but I'll watch you."

CHAPTER 28

JACK LAPOINT/CARLA COLLINS PORTER

He arrived in Carthage late, checked into the Days Inn. There was a note waiting for him. "Got the boat, I paid for it this time. There's a place in Quincy with all the fishing stuff. I'll pick you up at 9 a.m. Carla."

The next day was partly sunny, Jack could feel fall in the air, a little bit crisp when Carla picked him up. She met him in the lobby, they gave one another a harmless, platonic hug. He noticed she was driving a top-of-the-line Audi, appropriate for an heiress. They raced off to Quincy.

"Any more on the Hamilton case?" Jack asked.

"Not a peep. Sheriff's department doesn't have anything really."

"Much get out about it in the news?"

"Nothing really outside of the murder. Lots of the details haven't been released. None about the child porn."

"How's things in Boston?"

"Been kind of a rough patch. I got cited by the bar association for an ethics violation, but it's really just a payback jab from some attorneys on their board. Lost a girlfriend. She fell in love with a doctor at the hospital she works at. My doctor told me to start exercising, get in better shape. But all in all I've been okay, considering."

"You do look a bit thinner, Jack. I love exercise. You should try yoga, too."

"Hey, one step at a time."

"And you? What's been happening with you?"

"Same old, same old. The boys have been visiting, I've had a few interesting cases, nothing big, but interesting. I went to the doctor, too, because I wasn't feeling quite right. Turned out to be mild anemia. She told me to eat some liver. I tried, almost threw up."

"I love liver. Maybe I can get some tonight. I know a place in Quincy that specializes in chicken livers, scored carp as well," he said. Carla winced.

"Let's try Italian again, maybe that place in Keokuk?"

"Uhhh, yummmm. Spaghetti. That's where we'll go."

They picked up the boat in Quincy, almost identical to the one they'd had before. He bought a rod and reel, fishing license and tackle at the store on the riverfront, picked up bait. A half hour later they were cruising, temperatures climbing up into the low 70s.

"Let's go for some catfish today, or maybe carp. Trash fish, but they're fun to catch," he said.

They stopped alongside the banks up near Canton, the sky turning brighter, the temperatures climbing. It was going to be another great day.

"Mind if I put my swimsuit on?" Jack asked.

"Be my guest, I won't look," she answered.

Jack lowered his pants, underwear. Carla looked away.

"Okay, you can turn around," he said.

Carla then began to disrobe. Jack turned his head away.

It took a minute. "You can look now," she said. She was wearing the same one-piece she had before. She looked very pretty.

He set up his line, baiting the treble hook and casting it deep in the water with a big sinker. He decided to forego what's called "stink bait" to save both of them from puking. Even when he was a teenager he could hardly stand the smell, the product being well-named, actually made of rotting blood and guts from animals. The catfish loved it. He was using night-crawlers, messy but much better smelling.

"We'll just sit and wait now, see what's down there."

The two lounged in the sun, letting the river take them downstream. "No use putting an anchor out here, it won't hold, just drag us along and get caught on something."

About a half hour later the fishing rod jerked downward, Jack rushed to catch it before it flew out of the boat. "Oh, boy, it's a big one I hope!"

For the next five minutes he reeled the fish in, letting out line when necessary if the fish bolted. "You got to tire these guys out, eventually they stop moving around."

"Give me the net," he shouted when he saw something rise just below the surface. It was a huge gar, the prehistoric fish that looked half-snake, half fish, with a row of razor-like teeth a half-foot long.

"Oh, boy, I'm not bringing this guy in. I'm not even touching him."

Carla came over to the side of the boat to take a look. "Ooooohhh no, that's disgusting. Get rid of that thing."

He cut the line. "There you go buddy," Jack said. "Go back down to the bottom where you belong."

"Like I told you, lots of strange stuff in this river."

"Let's go do some boating," Jack said after he cleaned up the fishing tackle. He throttled up, they went way upriver, stopped the engine and let the river take over, floating downstream. They didn't even feel the need to talk, comfortable with the company, just drifting, watching, occasionally saying something. When you can sit with someone quietly and feel no need to fill the time with talk, that's special.

Later that evening they ate at the Italian restaurant in Keokuk. "I'm glad I only ate half that dinner," he said as they headed back into Illinois. "My doctor would be proud of me."

"Want to see the house where they found that guy over in Hamilton? It's just across the river."

"Sure, it'll give me a chance to digest my meal."

She drove across the bridge into the outskirts of Hamilton, taking back roads until they were about two miles outside of town.

"There it is, not a bad looking place. The guy must have had some money."

It was a two-story colonial, much like the ones scattered throughout New England. It sat up on a hill, looked to be about two acres of land.

There was a pickup truck parked way up the driveway. "Wonder who that is? I thought the place was still off limits until they finished their investigation," Carla said

"Turn around, let's pull up the driveway, maybe we can get a plate number. Might be useful later," he suggested.

"Hmm, Missouri plates," she said. Jack pushed the numbers into his cell phone, filed it away on his address book. "Maybe the sheriff can tell us who it belongs to."

Back in Carthage she drove him to the Days Inn. As he was getting out of the car she leaned over toward the passenger side. "Why don't you stay at my place tonight? It's got to be a lot better than this place."

Her apartment was stunning, she must have had the entire building renovated. Beautiful artwork arranged on virtually every wall, soft lighting enveloped the place, beautifully restored woodwork.

"It's not quite the Days Inn, but it should do for the night," he quipped. "You don't have an ice machine, do you?"

"You want something to drink?" She asked.

"Nothing, really, I've had enough for tonight. I think I'll just plunk down here," he said as he fell onto the plush sofa in the living room. "Ohhhh, this feels so good."

She sat across from him. "Tell me about this girlfriend who fell for someone else."

He explained how he had met Sarah, what she did for a living, how the two of them had what he termed a low-key relationship, as much about companionship as anything else. "She's good company but we both knew it wasn't going to be long-term."

"You ever have a relationship like that?" He asked.

"I haven't had a lot of relationships in my life, to be truthful. I dated a few guys before I got married, but nothing that got terribly serious. Then I married Peter. That was serious, at least on my part. He didn't take it as seriously. That's why we eventually divorced. I always came second in his life. I think my having the money made him feel inadequate, although he made a good living, too."

"We had a good first ten years, but after that we just sort of drifted apart, like a lot of couples do. You don't even notice it happening. You don't have the same friends, or any common interests. Then you're not doing things together, the excitement goes out of the marriage and then one day you wake up and you're a single person again," she said.

It was obvious she was growing tired, her eyes starting to half close as she continued to speak.

"Hey, I think it's time for you to hit the hay, Carla."

"Oh, I'm fading. Sorry."

"I'm ready to pack it in, too," Jack said.

Carla showed him the second bedroom, pointed out where everything was.

Sunday morning he rose early, before 5 a.m., went to the kitchen to look for the coffeemaker. He tried to be as quiet as he could, but Carla woke anyway. She stumbled out of her bedroom, shuffled over to the cabinets, went about making a pot of coffee.

"Not much of a morning person, Jack," she mumbled as she glided past him and back into the bedroom. "I'm going back to sleep."

He sat and drank several cups of coffee, looking around the apartment. He roamed around a bit, looking at the photographs of her sons, family members. The place was immaculate, unlike her desk at the courthouse. Obviously a very organized person, he figured. Her condominium was more feminine than her office.

Two hours later she came from the bedroom. He'd been showered and dressed for at least an hour, ready to go.

"Like I said, I'm not a morning person. Give me a minute to get my bearings. Any coffee left?"

"I made another pot. I'm afraid I'm highly caffeinated."

"What would you like to do today?" She asked as she pulled the curtains. "Looks like a fairly good day, a little cloudy."

"Well, I'd like to take a walk around town for one, see some of my old haunts. Then after that it's a totally free day," he said.

"Sounds good to me. I've got to stop in the office for a few minutes, then we can start our day. How about a drive around the county, see some sights?"

The day was leisurely, visiting several of the towns in Hancock County, Jack giving her a guided tour of places and events that occurred at various locations. The day grew colder and windy in the afternoon, the fall obviously upon them. It was a favorite time of year for Jack, be it either here or in New England.

"We'll just do dinner at the house, how about that?

"Great with me. Let's do something simple," Jack suggested.

They had a light dinner of stir-fry chicken and vegetables, shared a bottle of wine. They talked for a couple of hours, leisurely, naturally.

"I'm afraid I have to turn in. Got to get up early and make a couple of calls," Jack said.

He went to the guest bedroom. He was growing drowsy, turned out the bedside lamp. A few minutes later he saw a sliver of light as the door opened just a crack. Carla poked her head in.

"You interested, Jack?"

He made a place for her on his bed.

"Hello, Miss Collins Porter."

"Hello, Mr. LaPlant."

CHAPTER 29

HOWARD BOWLAND, MD

I've treated Jack for about twenty years now. He was one of my first patients when I started a practice here in Boston, just out of my residency at Mass Gen. We've kind of grown up together and although we aren't friends per se I know a lot about him because doctors get to know a lot about patients when they see them for that many years. As my practice has grown over that time and I started taking on partners, so did Jack. We're both probably at the top of our professions now. He's what I call one of my fun patients because we talk about all sorts of things.

My dad's the reason I'm a doctor, he's the one who hounded me over and over again to get my grades up and apply to the pre-med program at college. He wasn't a doctor so I couldn't figure out why he wanted me to be one so bad. He was an accountant at an insurance company. If it was up to me, I'd be nothing. Well, not nothing, maybe a guy who pilots a big ship or a lighthouse keeper or something. Sometimes I wonder what my life would be like if I worked at something else, like an airline pilot or engineer on one of those long trains that go out west and deliver coal.

People think oh you're a doctor and they call you doctor and they think it must be such an interesting job. It is in the beginning, but after time it's not so interesting. It's like painting a big bridge, the same thing every day and then you finish on one end and then it's time to start back up from the other end again. You hear the same things every day and see the same things all the time. You open the door to the exam room and there's the same flabby guy who doesn't want to see you but his wife nagged him enough that he finally dragged his ass in. Or it's the same woman with a whole shitload of ailments ready to dump out in front of you and she's not sick but lonesome and unloved and how do you write a prescription for that?

None of these people would ever think to ask me how I'm doing. I'm doing fine most of the time, but sometimes I have problems too like everybody else does.

Sometimes I'm bored out of my mind, even at home. I try not to let it show but it must come through sometimes. My wife says it's depression and I should see someone about it. But it's boredom, it's not depression, I know the difference. Besides, doctors don't go to doctors, we're invincible, hardly ever happens.

Every once in a while I get an interesting case and it breaks up the routine, strange stuff happens with the body and for no reason at all. The key is to ask a lot of questions, but that takes time and doctors don't have that kind of time, we're on roller skates most of the day seeing as many people as we can – that's how we get paid, for goodness sake. There was an old doctor I knew when I first started and he kind of took me under his wing. He told me that in all the years he had been treating patients the only thing that he could say for certain was that most people aren't as sick as they think they are, and the ones who are don't realize it.

The other day I had a fantasy that I would chuck my practice in Boston, cash out, take whatever money I had and go to Africa and set up a practice somewhere out in the bush, help all sorts of people with all those exotic diseases, the kind of doctor who sits in a hut with a stethoscope around his neck, wearing British-style military shorts and shirt, sweat pouring down my chest, like I was in some Joseph Conrad novel.

CHAPTER 30

CORNELIUS BONOMONO

I had a couple of very sticky situations on my hands and I really had to think about what to do. Because of my role with both the Irish and the Italian guys I was in a position to know a lot about what was going on in Boston. I had to be very careful to not just let loose with information that I knew. I had to keep neutral on a lot of things.

First thing was that Jimmy Olivetti was becoming a very big pain in the ass for the Italian side of the fence. I couldn't believe that at one time he'd been my friend and even my roommate. He was going off on his own and doing some independent jobs. One of them was about this guy who had a high tech company who Jimmy killed in a contract murder. Then there was the guy he shot who really hadn't done anything to him but piss him off by saying the wrong thing. That guy lived, but hardly. Sonny kept Jimmy around because sometimes Jimmy was valuable in solving a situation, and Jimmy Tracadora kept a close eye on him, but both of them felt that at some point in the future they may have to handle Olivetti.

Second thing was the fact that Jack LaPoint's partner was up to his eyeballs in working with Sonny and Jimmy Tracadora. I knew for a long time that Larry Maguire was on the payroll, and I had assumed that Jack knew but it never came up in any of our conversations because both of us never talked business with one another. But I found out through the grapevine that Jack had nothing to do with Larry's work for Sonny and Jimmy, he wasn't involved and knew nothing about it. In a way that made me feel better.

The problem was with Maguire. I'd heard through the network that Jimmy Tracadora had his doubts about Larry keeping closed mouth about all the things he knew about Sonny's operation. I was told that Jimmy wanted to make sure Maguire would never turn on them, so he took him out to a place where he killed a guy who had been talking with the feds about a hit that Jimmy Olivetti had done. He made Maguire watch him do it and told him that this was what happens to guys who aren't loyal. Jimmy Tracadora can be an animal, but it wasn't my place to say anything to anyone about how people went about their business. My role was to be neutral in almost all things, to keep the peace between the Italians and the Irish, and I did that. There were very few conflicts between the two and I have to pat myself on the back that much of that was due to my work.

My problem was whether or not to tell Jack about any of this. I decided I had to keep silent.

CHAPTER 31

LUCY WETTERAU

That place in Denver where I ended up was probably the best place I ever lived. I made a bunch of friends there and even got a little job down the street cleaning rooms at a little motel. I thought about my baby a lot and every once in a while went down to Littleton to see her. I had dreams about her, but she wasn't a baby anymore, but a full-grown person who you could talk to and she would talk back to me.

I stayed there for just under a year and it was hard to leave, but I had just enough money by then to get a small apartment with two other women who I knew from the shelter. I always thought that the word shelter was so good, because that's just what the place was, a shelter from the storm for us women. In the beginning you talk a lot about the men in your life who took advantage of you, maybe even beat you up, but after a while they fade into the background. That happens with all the women, after a while your life changes and those men fade away. You're not scared of them anymore, maybe not even pissed off.

I didn't do any drugs anymore, and that was so good, too. I started to get my shape back, and we walked everywhere because we didn't have but one car with the three of us. Shirley was one of my roommates, the one I was closest to and she and I would sit out on the back porch sometimes and laugh until we cried. She was from Colorado, but the part of the state that is as flat as Kansas, not the part where all the tourists go. Her dad was a farmer and he was the first guy in her life to slap her around, although he never did anything sexual to her. She went from guy to guy just like I did. I asked her once if she ever was with a guy who she really loved. She said no, then I told her what a jerk I had been when I told Jack that I was seeing another guy.

She told me that you can't look back in life, only forward. She was that way, always looking to the future and that's what I liked about her. She had what I would consider guts, that way of facing life head-on and not looking back. I wasn't quite that way, I'd look back and have my secret regrets and be sorrowful about them. She went with me to the cemetery one time to see my baby and she held me as I sobbed and sobbed. She didn't say anything to me, but just held me as I tired myself out crying. We got back in the car and drove to get a milk shake.

We all stayed together in that apartment for three years, helping each other out and pooling our money so we had pretty much for food, another car, and rent. One day Shirley told us that she was leaving, going back to the town where she was from. Her dad had died, her mom needed to go into a nursing home. The family still had a small farm and she was going back to see if she could make a go of it by herself. She had a brother in her hometown who said he'd help her out. She wanted to start an herb farm, to raise them and try to sell them in Denver. She wanted to raise a pig, too.

That pretty much broke up the group since Shirley was really the strongest of the three of us. After she left it really wasn't the same, and I started to get the idea that maybe I should move on too, do something with myself.

It's hard for a woman who's single. I still had my looks, so that was in my favor, and a lot of guys hit on me, but I wasn't really interested at that time. I met a guy who I kind of liked, he worked at the Denver zoo, but after we saw each other a few times he started to get real possessive, like some guys do, and that's a warning sign. I think he may have stalked me a few times, but after a while he went away.

I wanted another child, but I didn't really want to get hooked up with a man. That's a dilemma because I didn't think I could handle that, raising someone just by myself. The getting pregnant part would be easy to do, but the other part I knew I couldn't just do alone. That wasn't fair to the child.

All this time I had stayed away from alcohol. Every once in a while people would be drinking around me, and I'd look at the bottles and think, well, I can have just a little but something in me said no, don't take any of that, you'll end up where you left off, so I didn't do any drinking.

Eventually I got tired of Denver, maybe because it was hard without Shirley being around. I decided to go back to Illinois. On the way back to Carthage I stopped by to see Shirley, who had her herb farm. It turned out that I stayed with her for almost a year, helping her with some of the work. It was so much fun, and she asked me if I wanted to stay on, and I thought pretty hard about it. But being way out in the country far from any town seemed a little too lonely for me. It was perfect for Shirley because after all it was her home, but for me I needed more people around. On the day that I left we hugged for what was probably five minutes in the driveway of that farm, crying our eyes out. Then I got in my shitty little Toyota and drove away, headed east.

I didn't know if I was doing the right thing or not, but sometimes when you don't know what to do you head out somewhere else, hoping you'll find something good.

CHAPTER 32

CARLA COLLINS PORTER

There wasn't much I didn't get involved with in Hancock County, I saw the place as a book with a thousand different characters, and I was the narrator. It was like living in a play, only never knowing what the next act would be, what would happen or who would appear. Every day all you had to do was exist and something would happen.

It was like I went through a new door in a house and it opened up into a place I'd never knew could exist. That's what happened as my job as public defender started to expand. I saw myself as some sort of Joan of Arc fighting for the poor and the troubled. It was a reverie of mine, egotistical of course but it was my own little daydream. I couldn't ever see myself leaving Hancock County now, and I think that was the first time in my life where I was truly happy.

There was Jack, too, and that was really nice. He was a main character in the play, too, the guy who arrives on stage from time to time, the player who the audience welcomes every time they see him enter. I never knew whether I wanted him in a bigger role or not. Maybe later, but for now I was the director and I could decide at any time to change his role.

I had to keep reminding myself that this was Jack's home town, not mine. But it felt like I'd always been here, that I'd known this place since I was little. Maybe I daydreamed of a place like this when I was growing up, a place where I fit in perfectly, and lived my life on exactly my terms. Sometimes I felt guilty for feeling this good, this secure. I'd go to work at 7 a.m., two hours before most of the people got into the courthouse, and I loved the smell and feel of the place and I imagined what the people were like who had worked there over the years. I usually worked until about five, then went to one of my classes, usually at the gym, and then went home for dinner, or out with some of my girlfriends. We had a little group that got together all the time, at least a couple times a week and always on weekends for dinner or some outing. Brigette McNamara was probably my favorite, she was about my age and same kind of personality, fun to be around. She had started a bee farm – is that what you call a bunch of bees, a farm? No, hives. She started to sell her honey around the area, and it was a real business now. She had a pickup truck with the name of the company on the side – Brigette's Honey, of course, and she was just beginning to expand into the Quad Cities up north, and over into Peoria and over to Kirksville in Missouri.

Brigette had been married for more than 20 years to a guy over near Springfield, a guy with a pretty important job with the state Department of Transportation, but left him when she realized that her life had stalled out and that he didn't really care about her. Actually, technically she was still married, she just left him and picked out Hancock County pretty much like I did. She bought an old house on the outskirts of Carthage and started raising bees. Do you "raise" bees? No, you "keep" bees, that's right.

CHAPTER 33

JACK LAPOINT/CARLA COLLINS PORTER

Jack couldn't wait to get back to Carthage, felt like a teenager waiting to go to the prom with a new girlfriend.

He had to remind himself that this feeling had a familiar ring to it. He'd done it several times in his life, including with each of his wives -- head over heels, sprinting ahead before he should, making rash decisions. Maybe the distance was a good thing.

One night she phoned, her voice a different timbre.

"Somebody left a note on my car's windshield. It's a list of names, handwritten. Seven of them," she said.

"You know any of them?" he asked.

"They mean nothing to me. There's nothing else, just the names. The handwriting looks like a kid did it, but maybe like an adult trying to write like a kid."

"Take a picture, send it to me."

He looked at the note. It was from a page ripped out of a kid's school notebook, one side ragged.

The names – all apparently men -- meant nothing to Jack, either.

"Did you handle it much?" He asked.

"I put it in a plastic baggie. I'll get it over to the sheriff. It's probably nothing. But the sheriff or somebody over at the courthouse might know some of those names. Maybe they mean something," Carla said.

He asked Carla if the sheriff had chased down the owner of the pickup truck in the driveway of Garand's house in Hamilton.

"It's a construction guy over in Winfield County in Missouri, near Rhodes. No criminal record. They went to the house, the guy said he was there to do some work getting the house ready for sale. He's staying overnights when he works late. Sheriff called the relatives, it checked out."

"How about the "bees" those guys Buster or Billy or whatever?"

"Sheriff knew who I was talking about right away. He said they're drunks, users, not even able to organize a trip to the bathroom. And they had alibis for that night."

"You looking for company this weekend?" Jack asked.

"Well…let me see, I'll check my calendar…yeah, I think I can fit you in for a few hours on Saturday."

"Put me down for between 10 and noon Saturday."

"You're on," she said.

"It's probably too cold for the river, but maybe there's other stuff to do," she said.

"Let's make a trip up to Spoon River, up to Lewistown," he suggested.

"Great, I've never been there."

Spoon River is only two counties east from Hancock County. The river merges with the Illinois River outside of Lewistown. It's a small river, only about a hundred miles long, maybe 50 yards at its widest. It meanders, probably 12 feet at its deepest, clear water, sometimes all the way to the bottom.

They visited the cemetery where Edgar Lee Masters is buried, walking among the tombstones. Jack brought a copy of Spoon River Anthology, occasionally reading aloud some of the passages. Carla eventually stopped him.

"It's too somber. It's such a pretty day, let's just appreciate it. He talks about too many sad things."

She was right. He put the book in his sport coat pocket. They walked along the river, enjoying a lunch at a local restaurant that featured catfish and carp. Carla ordered salad.

They visited Galesburg, where Jack showed her Knox College, where he'd attended the final two years of college. They went to another cemetery, this one the location of Carl Sandburg's grave, another great poet and author from Illinois.

"We going to visit any other dead guys, Jack?" Carla quipped after they'd seen the grave.

"No, that's it for today. I have a bunch of other ones to see tomorrow."

On the way home Carla became drowsy, asked Jack to take over driving. As they drove into Carthage Jack swung the car onto the square near the courthouse. He heard a small crash in the window on the passenger side, Carla reaching up to her shoulder, crying out in pain.

Something had pierced her shoulder, shattered the glass on the Audi. He looked over, slowed the car, stopped. Carla was writhing in pain.

"Jack!" she screamed, "I'm bleeding!"

He looked at the window. It was shattered. He sped off toward the hospital.

He rushed Carla into the emergency room, yelling "She's been shot!"

The nurse hustled Carla onto a gurney, rolled her back into one of the emergency room bays. A doctor came running down the hallway.

The doctor and nurse worked quickly to exam the wound, giving Carla a local anesthetic in her shoulder. "Novocain," the doctor said, looking up at Jack.

"Looks worse than it is," the doctor said. "It's a bullet wound, I'd say. What happened?"

Jack explained what had occurred.

"Well, she's very lucky. The round must have lost some of its velocity."

Two sheriff's deputies arrived, along with an officer from the Carthage Police Department. They took statements from both Jack and a groggy Carla. The doctor gave Carla a Xanax to calm her down.

"I should be able to release her in a few hours. It's actually pretty minor, but definitely a bullet wound. No need for her to spend the night here. She'd be better at home," the doctor said. The nurse gave Jack instructions on how to change the dressing, wrote out prescriptions for Xanax, antibiotics, painkillers. "Carla uses Walgreens out by the bypass," the doctor said.

While Carla was being treated the police examined the car, took pictures, found a .22 round inside it.

"If you don't mind all the glass on the floor, you can drive it home," one of the officers told Jack.

Since the window had shattered it was impossible to get an estimate of the trajectory of the bullet. "We'll be combing the city tonight looking for any evidence, we'll be questioning everyone in that area to see if they saw or heard anything," a deputy said.

Jack drove her home with the window shattered, later wrapping it with a protective sheet in case it rained.

He put Carla to bed, sat by her until he was sure she was sleeping soundly.

She spent the following day in bed, Jack changing the dressing, administering the drugs, feeding her some very light snacks. "I think chicken soup fixes everything." He didn't leave her the entire day and following night. She slept most of the time.

"I have an idea," Jack said, sitting on her bed. "Why don't you get out of Dodge for a week or so, come with me to Boston. I'll set you up in an office and you can work from there if you want, or you can lounge around."

"I have so much work to do."

"I'll talk with the state's attorney, see if he can maybe open up the schedule a little bit to give you some recuperation time," Jack said.

CHAPTER 34

CARLA COLLINS PORTER

Jack introduced Carla to the other attorneys. She was transfixed by all the cases before them, all the tactics and strategies being discussed.

"Is it always like that?" she asked later.

"Pretty much, although I think there was a little grandstanding because you were there, you know, impress the visiting fireman."

"It makes what I do look so simple. Any one of those cases would break my back."

"You'd be surprised. You're probably doing a much bigger variety of things than anyone in that room, more than you realize."

"I know my clientele is very different. I don't think all of them combined could afford one hour from one of your attorneys."

"You're fighting the good fight. We're just whores."

Jack hosted a dinner to introduce Carla to his partners, their wives, and Brian McIntosh and his girlfriend Carol. It was on a Saturday night, the day before Carla was to return home. It wasn't a lavish affair, but he'd had it catered at his condominium.

Before the party began Carla came out of the bedroom in a stunning blue dress that covered the now-small bandage on her shoulder, a set of gorgeous pearls around her neck. He kissed her. "You look beautiful, you're going to put the other ladies to shame."

After about an hour of chit-chat, dominated by some hilarious stories told by McIntosh, a natural raconteur, the eight sat down to dinner as a couple of servers presented the first course.

"Carla, tell me about your practice," Ellen Stockwell said.

"There's not much to tell, really, I'm the public defender in Hancock County in western Illinois, we're located on the Mississippi. I'm afraid you could put all of our population into a few of the high-rises right here in downtown."

"Must be quite rural, cowboy and Indians kind of stuff," Sheila Maguire said, always one to make sure anyone from outside of Boston kept in their place. Cowboys and Indians, for God's sake, Jack thought.

"Actually, we don't have any cowboys left, even if there were any to begin with. That was a few states west of us, but we have quite a history. Indian settlements have been found there that could be as old as 10,000 years, and the county is where Joseph Smith founded the Mormons. He was murdered there, too, by a mob who stormed the jail where he was being held on bogus charges."

"Hmmm, interesting," Shelia said, "sounds quaint." Jack looked at Larry, smiled. What a bitch.

"Oh, it's quaint," Carla fired back with a slight sarcastic tone.

Leland changed the subject. "Carla, what do you think of Boston now that you've been here a week?"

"It's gorgeous. I actually went to school in Massachusetts, at Mount Holyoke. I've always loved the ocean, and one of the days I spent out on a tour boat, just taking it all in. It amazes me that men and women braved those seas in wooden ships to come here so long ago. It must have taken some strong stock to survive the winters up here."

The main course arrived, the talking withered as they ate.

"Jack, tell them about your adventure on the Mississippi when you were a teenager, you know, about the body you found," Carla said, giving Jack an opening.

He regaled them with the tale of Lucy and he finding the body, how the man's identity had never been uncovered. He went into a description of what it's like to be back in a slough, what a johnboat is, how powerful the river can be, the kind of stuff that can be found in its waters. He didn't tell them about Lucy except to say "a girl I knew."

He then told them the story about Edgar Lee Masters and Spoon River, why he was so attracted to the book.

"It's sounds so interesting. I've heard the name but not read any of his works," Brian's girlfriend Carol said. Jack got up from the table, fetched his small edition of Spoon River Anthology, handed it to her. "Here, give it a read, it won't take long. Keep the book."

"I think it's a rather bleak look at life," Carla chimed in. "I thought it too dark, pessimistic."

"That's our Jack," McIntosh interjected. "I've read the book, and a few others of his as well. His poetry is kind of haunting, even eerie." Jack wasn't aware that Brian had ever read any book. "There's another book I'd recommend if you like Masters, 'Winesburg, Ohio,' by Sherwood Anderson. They're both cut from the same cloth," Brian said.

The evening had been pleasant, enjoyable, except for a few edgy quips by Sheila Maguire.

That night, on the way to bed, Carla told him that her shoulder was feeling much better, that she was ready to return to Carthage and her pending workload. "Boston's very nice. It's a beautiful city. But I don't think I could live here, the weather's too cold for me, and some of the people are too. Not the ones here tonight, but others."

"I'm a Midwest girl, Carthage is where I belong, even though I just got shot there."

CHAPTER 35

FRANK STILLWATER

The Carthage police couldn't figure out where the shot had been fired that hit Carla. They canvassed that entire side of town, nothing was found, nobody had heard or seen anything. The best they could offer was that perhaps it was a discharge from some distance, a .22 capable of traveling about a mile. After all, it hit at a low velocity and there were always people in the county hunting down squirrels and rabbits or just shooting off their weapons. Despite that the fact of being hit by a bullet unnerved her. One of the cops noted that if there really had been an intention to kill Carla the shooter would have used a deer rifle, not a .22.

The names handwritten on the mysterious list that showed up on her car seemed to be a dead end, too. They were published in the local weekly newspaper, readers asked to contact the police if they knew any of the names. No one responded.

When Jack returned to Boston Leland Stockwell told him that Frank Stillwater had committed suicide. Jack had defended Stillwater a couple of years before on a charge of possessing child pornography, which was ironic considering Lucy's story. Even more ironic was the fact that Stillwater was the same guy who had fired Jack from his first job at the law firm, the pompous one who commanded him to go forth into the wilderness. Stillwater had hired Jack to defend him and their initial meeting was awkward, to say the least.

"Life's ironic, wouldn't you say?" Stillwater said. "Here I am years after I fired you, and I'm looking for you to save my ass."

"Bygones are bygones," Jack answered, looking across the table at the man who had changed Jack's direction in life. "Best thing that ever happened to me was you firing me. This firm wouldn't exist if you hadn't done that."

Naturally the charge drew tons of attention. If Stillwater had been just a working guy it might have been ignored, but he was now top partner in one of the most prestigious law firms in the city.

Any charge having to deal with child porn or pedophilia was devastating for a defendant, one of the only things left in society that carried with it the scarlet letter. You could be caught doing almost anything else but that charge was an instant career-ender. And that was just the charge, never mind the grand jury indictment or subsequent trial. Even if the charge was dropped or you were exonerated, it didn't matter. Friends fled, families went into hiding, people looked on in shock. In some countries even today those charges usually bring an instant execution, without benefit of trial.

Such was the case of Stillwater. One day he's riding in a limo on his way to the airport, the next he's vilified in the press, long-time buddies not calling him. Jack realized, of course, that in business so-called friends are usually not fox-hole buddies. It was like sharks, once you're wounded they often just leave you to die, or eat you up. Genuine friends who'll stick with you through thick and thin are so rare as to be almost non-existent.

Operating by his rule of never believing a charge, Jack worked on the assumption that everything was screwed up in the investigation. Stillwater maintained he was innocent of all the charges, that the stuff had been planted on his computer, although Jack really couldn't tell if he was lying or not. The man was despairing. The law firm disowned him, put him on unpaid leave until the case was resolved. Jack knew that even if Stillwater was found not guilty, the law firm would quietly pay him a severance, make him slither away.

The prosecution's case was simply okay, not airtight. They found on Stillwater's computer downloaded films and photos of children engaging in sex acts with each other, adult men. Jack detested having to watch these, but it was part of his job to see exactly what he was facing. How in the world do they find men who would produce and "act" in such films? Where do they find the kids and how do they coerce them into such things? How could men find this kind of stuff stimulating?

He had his buddy Barney Componari interview Stillwater, get a sense of the man, what he was all about. Barney visited Jack's office, closed the door behind him.

"I'll be frank. Frank Stillwater is a very disturbed man. I'm not saying he's guilty of what they're accusing him, but it's likely. He's a good liar, excellent as a matter of fact. He's suffering from the beginning stages of paranoia, suspecting all sorts of forces are out to get him. But as they say even paranoid people have real enemies. He's extremely competitive, but also self-delusional, believing he's smarter than the rest of us. He hides it well, but he's convinced of his superiority. Sexually he's a mess, but he won't admit it, just lets little things slip every once in a while that hints at a dysfunction in that area."

"Do you think he's a pedophile?"

"Probably," Barney answered.

"My hunch is that this guy is going to go right up to the wire, then finally confess or make a deal when he realizes his situation may be hopeless," Barney said.

"Is he suicidal?" Jack asked.

Barney thought for a minute. "Guys like this can break in half at some point, but some never break. Yes, he'd be on my list of guys who could kill themselves if he finally realizes the intense internal contradictions within himself."

This is what he both liked, and disliked, about his friend. On one hand he was rarely wrong, on the other he was rarely of use in his clients' defense.

"Let me ask you a question, Barney. Has this kind of stuff been around for a long time, child porn, using little kids for sex?"

"Been around since time began, I suppose. The game-changer is the web, it is oxygen to fire. It's virtually exploded worldwide. Before it was very clandestine, if a guy had these desires there weren't many conveyances for pictures, films, that sort of thing. My theory is that since it was so unavailable, a lot of these guys never had the opportunity to stoke their desires, get them hot. With the internet the whole scene changed."

"And if they did do something, and it was found out they were messing with kids in the neighborhood, everything was hushed up. No official reports were made, nothing in the newspaper. People just didn't talk about such things, a lot of people didn't even know such a thing even existed. The cops went to the guy's house, told him to get out of town, maybe beat the shit out of him, watched as they put him on a train, threatened to kill him if he returned. That's how it was handled."

"Now it's different. There's huge networks, rings of exploiters who know there's money in the business. And you know what happens when profits enter any picture," Componari said.

It was chilling, Jack thought. Add it to the pile of evidence that many human beings were awesomely evil creatures, barely kept at bay by a thin veneer of civilization, laws, rules, sanctions.

"What causes it?" Jack asked.

"A thousand reasons. Arrested sexual development. Physical and sexual abuse as a child, a warped view of erotica, you name it," Barney answered.

Barney was right. Stillwater maintained his innocence almost to the end, finally breaking down and agreeing to a guilty plea to a lesser charge if he submitted to an allocution in court.

After he heard the news of Stillwater's suicide, he asked his secretary to pull the case file on Stillwater. Jack then called Componari.

"You heard the news about Stillwater?"

"Saw it in the Herald yesterday, I was going to call you."

"You were right," Jack said.

"Unfortunately," Barney said.

The two spoke for a few minutes, agreed to meet later that week for lunch.

As Jack was handling Stillwater's file the folder slipped from his fingers and the papers scattered on the floor by his desk.

He began to pick up the papers and was halfway through the task of reassembling them when his eye just happened to hit upon one page in particular. It was part of a deposition taken before the trial. He half-read a paragraph as he placed it back in the folder and the name of Stephen Boylston was there. Funny, that matched one of the names on the list that had appeared on Carla's car in Carthage. Strange.

He read the deposition further. In it Stillwater had mentioned that he occasionally took vacations with friends, and Boylston was one of them he mentioned. It was irrelevant information at the time and only in Stillwater's later allocution did he testify to the court that those vacations had really been sex tours he went on in Thailand where men would be set up with young boys.

Jack phoned Carla immediately.

"What do you think?" Jack asked.

"Maybe coincidence, maybe not. But it's one hell of a coincidence," she answered.

"You think all those names are connected to a child sex ring?" Jack asked.

"Maybe."

The feds take cases of child exploitation seriously, so Jack forwarded to the federal court the list that Carla had given him, explaining to the judge from where it came, and what it probably constituted.

Stillwater clammed up when asked about Boylston. But it sparked an investigation of the names on the list placed on Carla's car windshield.

The feds were looking for a needle in a haystack, as the names matched literally thousands of men across the county. One name, Robert Clark, matched close to 2,400 individuals. Stillwater didn't seem to have any friends named Stephen Boylston and the ones they found around the country had no connection whatsoever to Stillwater. But Jack knew that coincidences like this don't just happen.

CHAPTER 36

JACK LAPOINT/CARLA COLLINS PORTER

"Just curious, but I assume you have a pre-nuptial with your husband when you married him?" Jack asked as the two of them had dinner at her condominium in Carthage. He'd flown in for the weekend.

"Funny you should ask that, Jack. I just got papers this week from his lawyer. He's contesting part of our agreement, saying it's too restrictive, that he's entitled to more of my money…I mean my great-grandfather's money, I didn't do anything to earn it except be born in the family."

"You going to fight him?"

"I don't know yet. It's not a lot of money he wants, I might give in to make it go away. I don't feel like going through any legal mess. The divorce was enough for me."

"You want me to look the papers over?"

"I don't want you involved at all, Jack. Don't take that the wrong way. I hope that doesn't insult you."

"Not a bit, I don't need any more work. Just remember that when people ask for a little bit more money, if they get it they'll ask again and again."

"I'm just being curious, don't infer anything about what I'm going to ask, but would you have me sign a pre-nup if we were to get married?"

"Why would you ask that? You looking to start a fight?"

"Just asking, like I said."

"The attorneys for the trust don't give me any choice. The trust protects the money from any interlopers who marry heirs."

"Just asking. My second wife signed a pre-nup, but I ended up giving her more than what she was entitled to, just to be a nice guy."

"This is just an academic question, right?" Carla asked.

"Purely academic."

The two smiled at one another.

"I guess I should have told you, the boys are driving over tomorrow. They called earlier and I couldn't turn them down. I want you to meet them, and them to meet you."

Her sons were both handsome, athletic types, but reserved with Jack, wary of their mother's boyfriend, as any children would be. The conversations were a bit stilted at first, minor chit-chat.

They spent the day in Carthage, having lunch at the condominium, going out later for a drive, with Jack taking a back seat with the one son, the other in front with his mother.

Jack couldn't figure out if he'd passed the litmus test with the sons. They left in late afternoon, the chit-chat never having become more than superficial. Obviously the jury was deliberating. Jack could imagine what the conversation might be in the boys' car as they traveled back to Champaign. "You think he's dating mom because of her money?" he imagined the first question that came up soon after they left Carthage.

"I think they're a little bit wary of me," he told Carla. "If it were my mother, I'd be the same way. They may think I'm seeing you just because of the money."

"Why would you say that? I thought they were very nice to you. You were very nice to them. I thought the day was fun. I think they like you."

"Just speculating, that's all. That's how I would think if my mother was wealthy and some guy shows up and started dating her."

In fact, one of the sons called his mother the next day, asking her just the questions that Jack had suspected were their concerns. She told him that Jack's intentions were honest, above-board. "He said he really liked both of you," she told her son. "Besides, he's got tons of his own money, he doesn't need any of mine."

Jack's attitude about money had always been a bit different than most people. He'd never been motivated primarily by money, although he was very satisfied with the fact that he earned quite a bit of it. When he started his practice in Chelsea it wasn't money he craved, but autonomy, to be rid of the need to work at a huge firm under the thumb of some moronic attorneys. He had never articulated to himself that someday he'd be looking out of the Prudential Tower presiding over a big law firm. It just happened to grow of its own accord.

He figured that when God cast Adam and Eve out of Eden, He invented money to make sure everybody would be miserable from then on. Greed figured in so many of the cases he handled, dominated much of the thoughts of many of his colleagues and friends.

Greed wasn't the only thing that drove his clients. Sex and power dominated as well. Susan Feeney was a great example. She was the cagey, manipulative wife of one of Boston's top financial executives. She'd been charged with deadly assault. Police said Feeney stalked a woman who she claimed was her husband's lover, and beat the holy shit out of her when the woman walked down an alley to her parked car. The single witness to the crime was a Mexican waiter who was about 60 yards away smoking a cigarette in the doorway in the back of a restaurant. Feeney allegedly used both her fists and an umbrella to smash the woman's face, break two ribs. She left the woman in the alley, calmly walked out of the alley and down the street to her car. The waiter claimed Feeney was the woman he saw beating the other woman. Jack thought he might be able to break that apart, as the waiter wore glasses, and the lighting in that alley at that time of day in overcast weather made it very difficult to see clearly.

It was a case perfectly fit for the media. Scorned wife beats husband's lover. Feeney was evasive, telling Jack that she was innocent, but offering him not much more than that. Jack thought it highly suspicious that Feeney just happened to find the one spot on the alley not covered by cameras to beat the woman. He found Feeney tolerable, but she wasn't someone he'd care to share dinner with, or even be around socially.

Feeney's husband was a creep. The victim was...well...a victim of both Feeneys, a thirty-something mid-level executive at the financial firm where Bruce Feeney was in charge. He scarred this woman emotionally, Susan left her marks physically. When the victim gave her deposition to Jack all he could feel for her was pity. If there was any real justice in the world the Feeneys should be placed in a dark alley and beaten senseless.

Why did so many men prey upon women? And why were so many women so susceptible to being conned by these powerful men? These women were highly educated, sophisticated, had great jobs with responsibility, yet they fell for the oldest lines in the book, "I'll leave my wife," still being the number-one bullshit line. Of course Bruce Feeney had used the exact line, the asshole.

The prosecutor had offered a plea deal, but Jack told her to reject it, claiming there were too many holes in the case. It went to trial and Jack tore the state's case to shreds. It took the jury less than an hour to find Susan Feeney not guilty. Innocent is not the same as "not guilty." Innocent doesn't have any legal definition.

CHAPTER 37

PETER

Things just never seemed to work out in the way I first thought they would. I first met Carla Collins Porter when she was with a bunch of friends down at a bar off Division Street in Chicago. We were all sort of drunk and it was late on a Saturday night and she was with a group of girls who were out celebrating with one girl who was getting married. I remember they were all laughing and my eye didn't really go to Carla first, but the girl who was the center of attention, the girl who was going to get married. I was with two friends and we all kind of mixed it up together and then I noticed Carla. She was the smallest of all the girls, certainly the skinniest, and she didn't do a whole lot of talking. I started a conversation with her and it wasn't about much, where she lived, where she worked, that sort of thing. It was so loud that I couldn't even hear many of her answers. She asked me a few things, too, like where I was from and where I worked.

I grew up in Chicago over in Oak Park and went to college down in St. Louis where I went to architecture school at Washington University. I liked St. Louis a lot but there weren't any jobs down there for architects, all the action was in either New York or Chicago. That's where all the sexy building projects were and I wanted to be part of that.

As luck would have it I ran into Carla six months later when I was going to lunch down on Wacker Drive after I got a job at an architecture firm. We looked at each other and I think both of us were trying to figure out where we knew each other. We stopped and pointed to one another and I asked her if she was the girl who was at that bar on Division. She was, and we smiled and started to talk. Out of the blue I asked her out and she said yes.

We started seeing each other and having lots of fun. I liked a lot of things about her. She was kind of an intellectual, liked literature a lot and that was something I was interested in. She was also very interested in the kind of work that I was doing. Her friends were fun, too, and I think she liked my friends.

It wasn't right away when I found out how rich she was. That didn't matter to me one way or the other but I did notice that she didn't have any money worries and lived in a really nice apartment downtown. She hardly ever talked about money but my friends were also joking with me that I'd hit the jackpot and to hold onto Carla for dear life. Like I said that didn't matter to me, we were having such a good time together, money or no money.

We finally decided to get married and oh what a big deal that was, that was when I saw the difference between my family and hers. Her mother organized the biggest damn ceremony she could. My family wasn't rich, but we weren't poor either and I'd never been around such fuss about a wedding. Carla kind of took a passive role in the whole thing, not fighting her mother. When I asked her about that she said it wasn't worth the battle, that let's have a big fun wedding. I liked her dad, he was a hell of lot more comfortable to be around that her mom, who I thought was kind of a cold bitch.

After we got married Carla got pregnant right away and we found out it was twin boys. Since Carla was so skinny and small it was almost hilarious to look at her as she expanded. At the end she could barely walk, but she did her best and the twins were born without much fuss, which is unusual for twins being born from a woman that small.

We moved up to Kenilworth which is the best of the best of Chicago, and we bought a beautiful house in a great neighborhood. I was rising through the ranks at the firm and now had a junior vice president position and I thought I was one hot shit. I was so busy in those days, trying to do all the work at the firm and racing home to be with Carla and the boys. We had so much fun in those days and I look back at those days now and realize that was the high point of my life.

Having tons of money, or at least access to a ton of money, isn't what people think it's like. It comes with a million strings attached to it. The money came from Carla's father side of the family, but her mother acted like she had earned it all herself and was entitled to everything. She was trying to stage-manage all of our lives, and it even drove a wedge between Carla and me. As the boys grew older Carla's mother tried to interfere with how we were trying to raise the kids.

Everything had to be the best, just perfect. Her mother just had to make sure that everything looked perfect on the outside, no matter what was happening on the inside.

When I was about forty five I got a part-time job down at the University of Chicago teaching design and architecture and I taught down there two nights a week. In the second year I was doing this I met Sandy who was studying to be a graphics designer and was a graduate student. She was older than the rest of them, I think 31 or 32 when I met her. It all started out just innocent but then one night when we were hanging out together after class she came up to me out of nowhere and kissed me. Oh boy did my life change after that. I remember driving home that night thinking what the hell had just happened, and then I got into bed and looked over at Carla and said to myself that won't happen again, there's just too much at stake here.

But there's something in humans I guess that makes them jump off cliffs, dive deep into the rock quarry and not worry about what might be below the water.

I got a small apartment downtown and Sandy and I were essentially living together and I hid it all from Carla. Then somebody told Carla about all of it and she called me late one night and it all came out. The next day her attorneys hit me so hard that I was spinning like a top.

CHAPTER 38

LUCY WETTERAU

After I left Shirley there in her driveway I drove away and ended up in Kansas City for about a year and a half and got a job cleaning motel rooms like I'd done back in Denver. I was kind of in a holding pattern, trying to figure out what my next step might be. That's a weird thing to be in, the space where you're sort of just drifting in your mind, kind of waiting for a sign from above about what to do, where to go. One night I went out and got real drunk and ended up sleeping with a guy I met at a bar. I woke up the next day about the middle of the morning and he must have gone to work or something. I just left his apartment and wandered back to my place. Later that day I thought what the hell, and packed the bag I had and drove east across Missouri and right into Carthage. I stopped in at the place where Rafe was working, and said hello, long time no see.

He was surprised to see me, and it was kind of awkward for both of us. I didn't really know what to say to him and he didn't know what to say to me. He still looked pretty much the same, maybe a little fatter. I could tell he was looking at me, too, and probably figured I must have looked pretty good, which I did since I hadn't been drinking or doing drugs for a long time.

It surprised me when he asked if I wanted to come back and live with him. I said yes right away. I don't really know how I felt about that just that I was back in Carthage and thought maybe we could make a go of it this time. We had a really good talk and I wondered if he had changed from the time before when he was drinking and even hit me a few times. He said he'd changed and he didn't act that way anymore.

We lived together for about five years and it was pretty good most of the time. Sometimes he didn't seem to pay much attention to me, but at least he wasn't drinking much, and I had a good place to stay and some stability. I got a regular job on the swing shift at the battery factory near the river outside of Hamilton, and I'd get home about midnight when Rafe was asleep. Sometimes I'd wait until three or four in the morning to go to bed, and Rafe would get up about six to go to work. We really didn't see a lot of each other, but it was a comfortable arrangement.

We actually tried to have a baby, but there was something wrong with me and I couldn't get pregnant. I went to see a doctor and he said that everything looked pretty healthy but mentioned that maybe it was Rafe who couldn't get me pregnant. I went home and told him that maybe he was shooting blanks and he got really upset and said it must be me, not him. I asked him how he was so sure of himself but he ignored me, said let's forget about the whole thing. I wouldn't let it drop and one night he did get drunk and told me the reason he knew he wasn't shooting blanks is that he got a girl pregnant in town a few months back. I started hitting him, screaming at him and he whaled off and hit me back, sending me to the floor right away. He said he was sorry over and over, but I went to my bedroom, packed my bags and left that night. There was a woman who I worked with who I called and I stayed with her for about a week before I got my own little apartment over in Hamilton.

CHAPTER 39

JACK LAPOINT/CARLA COLLINS PORTER

Carla was swamped by the mounting caseload of work in Hancock County, as more and more poor people found themselves on the other side of the law, or locked in fights with landlords, prison officials, state bureaucrats, banks, mortgage companies, repo companies, debt collectors. There didn't seem to be any end to the chaos. If she could devote an hour to an individual case every week that was a lot. Plus, her office became a gathering place for her clients, to the point where the county superintendent threatened to move her from the corner office on the third floor of the courthouse.

"Where did all these people go before this office was handling them?" she asked Jack.

"They didn't go anywhere, they just lived with their problems. Now that they have someone like you, they've come out of the woodwork. If you build it they will come," Jack said.

"I wish you could lend me a lawyer or two for a couple of weeks just to clear my workload," she said. "The minute I'm making headway another half dozen people trudge into my office looking for help."

"Do what you can, and then leave it at that. It's not like the county's paying you anything much. I think they're just glad to have you around, no matter how many cases you handle," Jack said.

"Change of subject. What's the latest on the second murder over in Hamilton?" Jack asked.

"Not a thing," she answered.

"Funny how that goes. You got two men with their throats cut and nobody knows a thing. You'd think in a town that small someone would know something, some little tidbit," Jack said.

Jack was fascinated by unsolved murders, ever since high school when he read true-crime mysteries. Also, it never seemed to stop astonishing him that people so often simply disappeared, or their bodies found scattered over the landscape, victims of God knows what. Even in Hancock County there were a handful of unsolved murders over the years, in a place like Boston or Chicago thousands of those cases. It was weird to think that if there are so many unsolved killings naturally it meant that there were many killers walking the streets free and easy.

At 3:13 a.m. on a Saturday morning something crashed through the window on the back bedroom of Carla's condominium, the one facing the alley. It was just loud enough to wake Jack, Carla still deep asleep.

"Carla, did you hear that?" he whispered. No response.

A little louder, "Carla, did you hear that!"

"Hmmmmm….what…what did you say?"

"I said something crashed. I'm getting up to go see."

She stirred a bit more. "Probably nothing, something fell over."

Jack walked slowly to the rear of the condominium, opening the door to the bedroom. He'd always been a chicken in situations like this, his heart pumping, him thinking there's got to be a half dozen bad guys in that room. Calm down he told himself, this place has security devices everywhere.

The window was cracked, a baseball-sized hole in one corner. On the floor was something. He bent down, picked it up. It was a rock with a paper wrapped around it with string. He looked outside from different angles, trying to see if anyone was still there.

He took the rock with the paper attached into the kitchen, turned on the light, undid the string. A note, in kid's handwriting. "Lucy was innocent. Those guys needed killing."

Carla was up now, watching Jack. "What is it?"

"A note. Attached to a rock someone threw through the window." He showed her the note.

"As they say, let's go to the film," she said, "I had a camera installed front and back after that shooting."

"You never told me that, Carla," Jack said.

"Yes I did, right after I got back from Boston. I told you I was going to have a surveillance system installed. You probably weren't listening," she said.

She opened a small box in one of the kitchen cabinets, removed a gadget that she then hooked up to the television. She used the controller to guide the video forward until it came to the present date. She slowed it down to review the past half hour. She sped it up until a figure appeared, threw the object toward the window. The figure was shrouded in a hoodie, impossible to tell even whether it was a man or woman. The figure walked slowly away from the scene, toward another alley that led away into another street. In less than a minute the tape caught the glow of what were probably headlights, but the car never appeared on the video. Maybe they knew they were being filmed.

"That person threw like a girl," Jack commented, "or a guy who throws like a girl."

Jack examined the note.

"I'll call the sheriff," Carla said.

CHAPTER 40

SHIRLEY

I don't live near the interstate but I see it every once in a while when I go into Waverly and it's always crowded with cars and trucks coming and going from Denver. Keep moving, I tell the traffic, pass by this place and keep on going, I don't want you to find this place. This is eastern Colorado and we're just flatland and boring and you want to keep going to the mountains.

After I hugged Lucy when she left that morning I just sat down by a big tree in my front yard and cried and cried. I just knew that would be the last I'd ever see of that wonderful woman and for some reason I knew that she'd have a bad end eventually. Some people are just doomed and she was one of them, so vulnerable that it's just tragic. I guess I was one of her protectors and when we lived together it seemed that I was always lecturing her to make sure to do this, do that, stay away from that situation, stick to the straight and narrow. But she had an innocence about her and a sweetness that you just don't find very often. She was flypaper and catnip both together for shithead guys who treated her badly. That was kind of a problem for all of us at the shelter but somehow I toughened up and got wise. Lucy didn't.

My herb farm was doing very well, and I think my brother had doubts about it but now he was in the business with me and we made some deals with stores in Denver and over in Wichita and we were selling our stuff regularly. We even had an internet business and it was doing really well, too. My mom had finally died in that awful nursing home down in Waverly and the house was free and clear, my brother and I owned it outright. A lot of people thought it was kind of lonesome the way I was living, out in the country and pretty far from any of the small towns, but I was as happy as I'd ever been, didn't seem to need a whole lot of company. But even Lucy wouldn't stay around because of the isolation. Me, I didn't see it that way, enjoyed every morning I woke up and saw the big great horizon outside my window and thanked God that such grace was bestowed on me.

Lucy got in touch a couple of times to tell me that things had settled down, and that she hoped this would be permanent. She was back in the small town in Illinois where she grew up and working at some factory. But way back in my mind I had this feeling that things never went very well with Lucy for a very long time, and I used to say a prayer for her at night before I fell asleep. Why did God sometimes punish the sweetest people?

CHAPTER 41

LELAND STOCKWELL

Things weren't going right at the firm. It wasn't about the business itself, it was still making lots of money. That wasn't the problem. My partners were the problems, we seemed to be floating free of each other, the bonds that had kept us together starting to unravel. Something was happening to Larry and I couldn't figure it out. He was distracted, or depressed, or something. I even went into his office and closed the door behind me and asked him what the hell was bothering him. He said it was just mid-life shit, coping with his kids and his wife and all the other pressures we all have. He said he was taking care of things one by one and was feeling better about everything, that he didn't see any problem affecting the firm. I took it at face value and hoped for the best.

Leland was another matter. I wasn't as worried about him but he just didn't seem to have his head in the game like before, he was making mistakes that he never made before. I had to kind of pussy-foot around him to see what might be wrong. I asked him out to lunch one day and we kind of shot the shit about a lot of things and finally I had to ask him if anything was bothering him. His answer surprised me and he told me that he was gay, had always been but just buried it and got married to a woman but that he'd fallen in love with a guy downtown who worked at another law firm. I knew the guy, and knew he was married to a woman, too, and had kids.

Leland said he'd come to the decision to come out of the closet. I was surprised, but got back on my pins right away and told him that so much had changed in the past thirty years and that being gay was nothing to be ashamed about, not like it was when we were kids and if anyone found out you were gay you'd be a pariah.

I don't know if he felt any better having me say that but he said how in the hell was he going to tell his wife and kids? I told him that I couldn't give him any advice and that was all his own decision but I did tell him that I got his back on anything he does. I asked him if Larry knew and he said no he'd not told him yet, that I was one of the first he'd told. I said I was flattered by that.

I have seen law partners change all the time. The names on the firm sometimes didn't relate to anyone who was actually there anymore, just names on a wall with maybe a few old portraits on the wall of old guys. Or firms just fold all the time. People think that law firms are like regular companies, but they're not, they're very loose associations of men and women who come together but it's more like cattle in a field, each one grazing in their own spot, coming together every once in a while to stand under a big shade tree to talk over the day.

I pretty much expected that LaPoint, Maguire and Stockwell would run its course eventually after we all got old and rickety. I gave the firm maybe five years if it was going the way it was now. I figured that Leland would find a new life and that Larry would do, well, whatever he was going to do. I could feel myself moving ever so slowly out of Boston and back to Hancock County, to Carla. Hey, nothing's forever, even though sometimes we want it to be.

CHAPTER 42

LUCY WETTERAU

When do you know that your life is over? I don't mean the kind of over like dead and buried, but the kind where you know you'll just sort of occupy space until something happens to kill you. Maybe not tomorrow, or next year, but maybe five years down the road. That's how I felt over in Hamilton, like a zombie or something. I knew I'd never have a child, I still thought about my little girl lying in a grave in Denver, about the men in my life who were no good, drunks and druggies who always turned on me. What was in me that made me make such shitty decisions about men? Every once in a while I would think of Jack and wonder what he was up to now. I heard only a couple of things about him during the years I lived in Hamilton, a couple of people who we went to high school had heard that he was a big-time lawyer in Boston, that he was married and that he had a son. I could just imagine him in a big office, surrounded by nice things, going home at night to a big house with a bunch of lights on, and dinner waiting on the table, him kissing his wife and hugging his kids.

The battery factor closed up and we were all thrown out of work. I tried to get a job over at the Mormon complex in Nauvoo but there were so many people looking for work that I never had a chance, they wanted people with clerical skills and at least a few years of college. I was running out of money and was way behind on my rent. I had a girlfriend who was in the same boat, and we decided to live together to save money. Her name was Ann Campbell and I decided to live in her apartment down by the river in Hamilton, really kind of little place that didn't charge much money. We both got jobs cleaning houses and we pooled our money, but it still wasn't enough. We applied for welfare, but didn't get much because we weren't making below the minimum they required.

Ann told me one night that she had an idea and for me not to get insulted if she brought it up. She said it was only an idea and maybe she wasn't even serious about it, but it might be a way to make some cash and not have to pay any tax on it. I told her to tell me the idea, but I had an idea beforehand what it was about.

We were both fairly good looking still and still had pretty good bodies, and she said why don't we start out like offering guys blow jobs? She said what we could do is let some of the bar owners near the river know that we were available if they knew guys who wanted something like this.

I told her I had to think about that and maybe there were other ways to make money. I told her that it may start out giving blow jobs, but men would want more than that, and then we'd be in a fix. I told her I'd think about it.

It didn't take very long for me to decide because the work cleaning houses began to dry up because the economy got real bad. Ann said it was probably time to start our new business, and that we could do it in the apartment bedroom. We agreed that the other one would be in another room to make sure nothing got out of hand.

We got our first customer, an older guy who heard about us at the Riverboat Tavern on the river. He came to the house, and Ann was the one to handle him. She took him into the bedroom and ten minutes later he left, and Ann had a crisp $20 bill, with a $5 tip. She smiled at me and said it was a good start.

The next day I took care of another guy, and got $20 but no tip. He was an okay guy, but not too clean. I had to take a shower right after he left. After about three weeks we'd made a lot of money as word got around and our prices went up. Deckhands from the river barges were pretty much a steady business, horny guys who just got off the boats and needed to be taken care of. There wasn't any trouble at the apartment, and we decided that maybe we could take two at a time.

Like I said to Ann the guys wanted more than just blow jobs and this I had to think about. That's a whole new level of business, and with it comes risks of disease and you have to take precautions. A lot of guys didn't want to wear rubbers, and there'd be arguments about that. Some guys were rough, or drunk, and that was another problem.

We did this for about a year and a half, not all the time, but when we needed the money, and we made pretty good money. We got another apartment, a bigger nicer one this time. Life was okay, except for one thing. To keep doing what I was doing I needed something to help me keep up with the work. I started doing cocaine again, not much at first, but it gave me the push I needed with the guys.

CHAPTER 43

ANN CAMPBELL

It wasn't something I set out to do, just an idea I had after the battery company shut down and left us all high and dry. I really didn't even think of it right away and I never had a plan ready. I talked with Lucy Wetterau about it and the idea kind of grew from there.

The family I grew up in was kind of screwed up. My dad tried to molest me once when I was about ten but even at that age I knew it was weird and got away from him and I told my mom about it. She got real quiet I remember and asked me where and when it happened. They had a big fight that night and my dad started hitting my mom but she was ready for that and had my little brother's baseball bat by the side of the stove and she hit him really hard just once in the kneecap and he fell to the ground screaming his head off. Then she called 911 and told the cops he tried to have sex with me. They carried him out of there and off to the hospital. She'd busted his kneecap really bad and he was never in my house again, and I only saw him around town a couple of times and then he vanished. My mom was like that, once you pissed her off you were on her shit list for life. If she had had a shotgun instead of a baseball bat that night she would have blasted him into eternity.

Lucy and I had a real good thing going after the battery factory. We were up to handling a half-dozen guys a day on a busy day, making really good money. We got along really good and I liked Lucy a lot. She was kind of sad I thought and she told me about the guys who took advantage of her in the past and her little baby dying at birth. I cried so hard when she told me that story. I could never get pregnant and my doctor said that was probably permanent.

We did that for a couple of years and then I wanted to get out of the prostitution business. That's what I told Lucy, but it wasn't really the truth. The truth was I met a guy and he asked me if I'd like to make some porno movies. He told me what was involved and the money I could make which was more than I was making with Lucy and me working together. He made the films right from his house there in Hamilton and I did those for about two years but quit because this guy wanted me to do weirder and weirder stuff. He was selling his films and I always wore different wigs in them so I wouldn't be recognized, used different kinds of makeup to hide what I really looked like. It was time for me to do something else besides sex. When I told him that I wanted to quit it didn't bother him much because he said I was losing my looks anyway and getting flabby tits. I got a job at a car wash over in Keokuk and that was fine with me.

Lucy never found out I was making porno films or if she did she never mentioned it to me. I only saw her from time to time and she just seemed even sadder to me, like life wasn't worth it. I saw her once with a guy who I knew from the porno work, a guy who did the lighting stuff. He was blind as a bat and a really creepy guy. Lucy and this guy were both drunk and hanging off of one another. I waved at Lucy and she waved back but I think she was so drunk she didn't know it was me.

I got to know a guy in Keokuk who worked at the car wash and he knew another guy who he said might be good for me. It turned out he was nice to hang out with and he treated me right. We had some fun together and I decided to move in with him, he had a house on a hill overlooking the river that he said was his mother's and that he had gotten when she died. He told me one night when we were drinking that he heard about these guys over in Hamilton making porno movies and I got real uptight when he started talking about it and maybe he knew I was part of that operation at one time.

I didn't let on that I knew about it, and just let him talk. He said he'd heard that the guys making those porno movies had even made a snuff film with some teenage runaway. That got my interest right away but I thought no that can't be true, not the guys I worked with over there. But he said that a friend of his had seen the film, and it sure looked like a snuff film. They put a gun to the girl's head and they fired it and blood went everywhere. I'm thinking this is all made up, this "I got a friend business," sometimes you hear that and just know it's not true.

Then he says that this friend of his says one of the guys that works on these films works out of his house in Hamilton and he's got a guy working for him who's almost blind, real thick glasses. Then he tells me that they're also doing kiddie porn stuff, getting kids from all over the Midwest and either bringing them to Hamilton, or going to film them other places. They got a few guys who are in the films with these kids, and that they're really disgusting.

A few days later I got ahold of Lucy, and found her in a bar down by the river. It was earlier in the day and she wasn't drunk yet, so she was making pretty good sense. I told her about what I'd heard about the snuff film and the kiddie porn business, said I'd heard it from a friend and I was warning her to stay away from this guy that I saw her hanging out with.

She seemed really surprised and said this guy was really nice to her, that he was treating her pretty good and I got out of her that he was feeding her free drugs so that's why I figured she thought he was a nice guy. I warned her again to stay away from him, that he was no good and the stuff he was wrapped up with was dangerous. I looked her right in the eye and told her all this.

CHAPTER 44

LARRY MAGUIRE

They started to turn the screws on me more and I knew I was way over my head but there was no way out of this maze with Sonny and his mob guys over on the North End. I'm sure that the FBI or the police knew I was involved with them because they always keep these guys under surveillance. Most of the time we had to communicate outside in some park or other place and when we talked inside anywhere it was always in code. I had been working with these guys for so long I couldn't help but knowing most of the stuff they were up to, who they'd probably killed and who was on the take and what operations they were involved in. They didn't even pay me much because they knew I was a house captive, what could I do, ask for a raise? It wasn't like it was corporate America. The money had always come in handy, extra cash for helping to pay for tuition or a new car or paying off a mortgage. We were living well. I didn't tell a soul about my work for these guys, not Sheila, not Jack, not anybody. Jimmy Tracadora made sure by killing that guy in front of me that my loyalty would be guaranteed.

One day a guy called my secretary and said he'd like to make an appointment with me over some trouble he'd gotten into with the feds downtown on a racketeering charge. My secretary booked an appointment for the next day, but I didn't have much time open so she gave him only a half-hour. He walks in my office and he's a sight to behold, he looks like he's wearing his pajamas and he even smells. Oh, God, this guy won't be able to pay, he looks like an unmade bed.

He goes into this litany of legal problems that he's in and I start taking some notes. He says don't worry he has the money to pay for all of this, and would cash be okay? I tell him that we want checks to make sure there's documentation of payment, then he tells me out of the blue that that's not what he understands from the boys in Sonny's mob, he hears from them that I often work on a cash basis. It floors me that he knows about any of that, I thought they were as closed-mouth about it as I was, and I knew this guy wasn't connected with them in any way, I'd never heard of this guy.

Then he gets all serious on me and calls me Mr. Maguire and leans forward on his chair and puts his hands on the opposite side of my desk. He says that he's with the FBI and that he knows all about me and my work for the mob, that they've been tracking me and that they have me dead to rights and maybe I'd like to work out a deal or face charges of racketeering, tax evasion, and complicity in about a half-dozen murder investigations. I felt my stomach clamp up and my bowels loosened. I could tell the blood drained from my face and I even got a little dizzy.

He told me that all this legal work he wanted me to do for him was legitimate. He was undercover deep and he really was charged with all this racketeering stuff, but he was an FBI agent. He wrote down a cell phone number and said think about it but what he wanted was for me to become an informant. I told him I didn't know what the hell he was talking about and play acted like I was shocked at what he had just said. He said he'd be back in touch very soon. He left the office. I went to the bathroom and sat on the toilet for fifteen minutes, shitting my brains out and wondering how the hell could I get out of this horrible situation? Maybe this guy was a plant from Sonny's gang, sent in to just test me to see if I was willing to rat them out. If I said yes to this guy then they'd kill me. Or maybe he really was a fed and if I didn't work with them they'd hang me out to dry, and I'd lose everything, everything I'd worked for over all these years. Sonny's gang had me a lot more scared than the feds could ever scare me, so I decided to get ahold of Jimmy Tracadora and tell him about this guy who came to me and said he was an FBI agent. I figured that if he was a plant from the mob that it would prove my loyalty.

CHAPTER 45

LUCY WETTERAU

So just out of the blue one day Ann tells me that she's getting out of our business, that she wants to do something else. We had a good thing going but I didn't think I was going to be able to do it alone. She was my partner and without her I didn't think I could do it day after day. I was getting sick of the guys and what I did to make a living, besides business was falling off anyway, maybe because I was getting older and not as pretty as I used to be. Don't get me wrong, I was still good looking but maybe not like I used to be.

Ann and I kind of went our own ways and I had to find a job to support myself. I found a part-time job at Wal-Mart over in Keokuk, and I worked there for about three years until they caught me one time with liquor on my breath and the boss fired me right on the spot. That and some public assistance was what I was living on, so I had to figure out what to do next. I got a job at a couple of taverns in Hamilton, just cleaning up tables and doing some kitchen work out back like washing dishes and things. The pay was shitty, but it was all I had. Instead of an apartment I got a room in a rooming house down a ratty old street in Hamilton. I had to give up my car, so I was on foot most of the time, even when I had to go to the grocery store which was about two miles away.

I saw Ann every once in a while and she said she was doing well, that she got some work over in Keokuk and was supporting herself pretty well. She looked pretty good to me, at least better than I thought I looked, but then again I was always a few years older than her anyway.

When I wasn't working I was in my room watching television, or reading books. It was the first time in my life when I was interested in reading and I even got a library card and went there every week and got a book out. It was fun and I wished that I had picked up the habit earlier in my life. I think during those days I didn't talk to many people and I had a lot of trouble sleeping. I wasn't even interested in eating too much and I read that these might be signs of depression. I went to a doctor and they examined me and he said I should go see a counselor or a psychologist. But I didn't have the money, so I sort of diagnosed it myself and decided that it was probably depression and that maybe it would go away on its own. Some of it did, but not all of it.

I met Eddie at one of the bars where I worked and we got to talking. He seemed like a nice guy, friendly and maybe a little lonely, kind of like I was too. We'd have a drink after my shift was over, and then maybe go to another bar after that. We'd go to his apartment since mine was so shitty and we'd talk a bit and then watch some television. Every once in a while we'd have sex but it was kind of hard with Eddie because he had a problem keeping it up. He also had a big problem with his eyesight and he wore thick glasses and he would run into things from time to time. But he seemed like a real nice guy.

Eddie told me he did odd jobs around town, that's why he had money pretty much all the time. I never asked him what he did, but I thought maybe it was about drugs or something like that. He didn't talk like a pusher, although one night at his apartment he had some cocaine in a drawer and asked me if I'd like to do some. We did and had a good time.

We started to do cocaine a lot, several times a week at least, and we'd have little drinking parties either at the bars or at his house. Sometimes he'd have a couple of his buddies over and maybe another girl or two and we'd party. Sometimes someone would bring some heroin or pills over, too, and we'd do those things, too. I knew I wasn't going in the right direction, but I just couldn't help myself and I thought oh what the hell.

One time Ann came to see me and told me to watch out for Eddie and his friends, that a friend of hers said they were into bad things, making films where they killed a girl and films with sex and little kids. I didn't know what to tell her, that nobody ever mentioned anything like that to me, that I would have known since I spent a lot of time with Eddie. She told me to keep away from them, that they're dangerous. I was just confused because I knew Ann so well, trusted her and didn't ever know her to make things up.

Eddie and I kept on our partying either just the two or us or with his friends, too, and one time when we were really high, just him and me alone, I asked him if he knew anything about porno films or kiddie porn or that stuff. He just laughed it off, says where would you hear such things, and then he just let it drop. I let it drop too, thinking Ann was wrong about all that stuff.

Then about six months later we were stoned out of our minds and Eddie said to me that he was helping to film some of the porno, that there were some kids involved, but it wasn't very serious. He said he liked kids, but I realized later that what he meant was that he liked kids in a sexual way. It kind of disgusted me, but still Eddie was good to me, never did anything to me. I'll say though that by this time Eddie was the guy who gave me drugs, all for free, and that's what I really wanted, I'd do anything to keep that coming since I had no way to buy drugs myself. He treated me right, and that was it. We never talked again about those films.

CHAPTER 46

LARRY MAGUIRE

I was still in the men's restroom after my meeting with the undercover agent and I thought it all over again and decided not to tell Jimmy Tracadora about the feds contacting me to become an informant. I thought if I told him that he'd kill me anyway, just to make sure I never talked. He wouldn't kill me right away when I told him, but the way he worked I knew he'd make me feel good about coming to him first, and then he'd kill me or have someone kill me the next day or the day after that.

I couldn't even be sure that the guy who had walked into my office was the real McCoy or not.

The FBI undercover guy, or whoever he was, would be back in my office soon, I knew that, and I still didn't know if he was for real or not, so what I decided to do was disappear. The only problem is that it's almost impossible to disappear, I had to have a plan and I had to follow through on it really soon because I knew I was between a rock and a hard place, maybe even worse than that because I was much more afraid of Sonny and Jimmy than I was of the feds, if they really were the feds.

I thought to myself that to really disappear you'd have to go up to the top of the Prudential Building and be abducted by aliens. I had heard of cases where people just disappear, a guy goes out to buy a gallon of milk and nobody ever sees him again. I needed to be that guy.

Here was my ace in the hole. About five years ago I started to put money away in a safe deposit box and I can't tell you why I did that except that I thought there might be a day when I'd need it for an emergency. Maybe I thought then that I needed an escape hatch just in case I got on the wrong side of Sonny. But then when I started to get really paranoid about Tracadora and Sonny I got to thinking that maybe there would come a time when an emergency came up and I couldn't get to the safety deposit box so I took all of it out and put it in my safe at the office. I had about $25,000 in $100 bills, and almost 100 gold Krugerrands.

I said to myself that I had to really think this thing through so I closed my office door and put my brain to work. Keep it simple I told myself, don't make it very elaborate.

I had a brainstorm. I had to disappear immediately, as in that day, in a few hours even. I got up from my desk and looked out the window and figured here's what I'd do. I'd not leave one trace of myself. I couldn't go to the parking lot to get my car, and I couldn't be picked up on any cameras that were all over the place. I'd leave my office, just like I was going home, and I'd make sure someone in the office saw me leave. At least they'd see me head to the elevators. But I had to figure out how to escape the building without being picked up on a camera.

Then I sat down and wrote a letter by longhand to Jack and Leland, and a separate letter to Sheila that they were to deliver to her, and I put them in my safe. On a sticky note I wrote the combination to the safe and walked over to Jack's office and put it on his desk, nothing but the numbers.

CHAPTER 47

ANN CAMPBELL

I saw Lucy one day and she was so fucked up I couldn't believe it. I walked right up to her and she lifted her head but honestly I don't know if she knew who I was or not. She was like a zombie. I had to shake her to get her attention, tell her it was me, didn't she recognize me?

Eddie must be giving her drugs all the time, I figured. He was such a creepy guy, I always thought that, and now he was feeding enough drugs to Lucy that it would kill her. Her hands shook, she smelled and I doubt she got one meal a day, the flesh just hung on her body, and here she'd been such a pretty woman before when we worked together.

It was no use talking with her and she just went on her way down the street in a daze. That woman wasn't long for this world if she continued this way. I thought I'd like to kill Eddie.

I was still with that guy in Keokuk and we had a regular relationship going, it was nice. We were both making some money and pooling it so we could have some luxuries like a nice car and a weekend away once in a while. He treated me very well, and had manners, even getting the car door for me and he even once bought me some flowers for the house. I thought this might work out for the long run.

He mentioned one night that he heard some more from his friend about that operation over in Hamilton and he said that his friend had gotten a copy of some of it. He told his friend he wanted nothing to do with it, didn't even want his friend to show him that shit. I thought maybe I should check it out, not because I had any interest in it, but I wanted to find out if what he said was true, that the guys I used to work with were doing kiddie porn or even this snuff film business. I told my boyfriend that I was curious about this, that I didn't believe they were making such things and that I needed to see some of it just to verify if the rumors were true. He thought I was crazy but I told him I thought the whole idea was disgusting, but I needed to know for myself.

He arranged for me and him to go to his friend's house but said he'd have nothing to do with any of it, he'd sit in another room while I watched some of it. We did that and his friend took me to a computer and put a DVD in. Immediately I knew the rumors were true and saw some truly disgusting and depraved things. But what really spooked me was I could tell that the filming had been done at that guy's house in Hamilton where I used to do porno films. About three minutes into the film I noticed that the camera went a little haywire, maybe got a little bit rocked by somebody hitting it and out of the corner appeared just for a second the face of Eddie. I had this guy shut the computer off, thought to myself I got to get out of there. I almost ran to my boyfriend in the next room and told him we got to go right away. Once we were in the car I told him that he had to get rid of that friend who showed me that film, and that if he didn't I'd leave him. He got the message, and promised to never see the guy again. He knew I was serious as hell.

In the next couple of weeks I knew I had to do something. I was crazy with worry for Lucy and bullshit with anger and hate for Eddie and the other guy I knew who was making those films. I had no doubt they were capable of making a snuff film, and for all I knew maybe Lucy was going to be the next victim. I could barely do my work at my job for all I was thinking about it. I slowly came up with a plan.

I went out a couple of nights and looked over where I knew Eddie lived. One night I even went up to his door when he wasn't home and checked it out. What a rat hole. I tried the front door and found that he hadn't even locked it. The next night I happened to drive by and saw that he was home, lights on in the front room and I could actually see him in the chair with the television set on.

One night I told my boyfriend that I'd be working the overnight shift and wouldn't be home till early the next morning. I drove over to Hamilton and parked my car near Eddie's house. I saw him coming home, and knew he must be drunk. I waited maybe an hour in the car, then got out and slowly went to the house and peeked in the front window. He was asleep in the chair. The front door was unlocked and without giving it a thought I walked right in and drew the shades on the window and pulled from my coat jacket a big kitchen knife and I sliced Eddie's throat wide open. He didn't even move from the chair, he barely opened his eyes and I watched the blood flow right down from him into the carpet. Goodbye shithead. I wiped the handle of the blade with a cloth and dropped it on the floor. I went through his pockets and only found some loose change and a small little scratchpad notebook. I took the notebook. Lucy wouldn't be in danger anymore, at least not from this guy.

When I got home my boyfriend was just getting up for work, and we had coffee together and I told him that I was going to go right to bed because I was so tired. After my boyfriend had gone I called 911 on a throwaway phone and told the dispatcher there was some screaming at Eddie's address. I crushed the phone and threw it away.

I went out of my mind crazy when I heard that Lucy had been arrested for killing Eddie Crane. I had no idea she was in the house but I figured what must have happened is she was in a bedroom and woke up and found Eddie in the living room and then the cops came because I had called them. What the hell was I going to do, I couldn't very much walk into the police department and say it wasn't Lucy, it was me who cut Eddie's throat. I was going crazy about what I should do, but I just sat tight, see what would happen to Lucy.

I heard on the radio that Lucy was at the county jail over in Carthage and I thought maybe I'd go to see her, she how she was doing, but I thought maybe they could trace me back to the murder somehow if I appeared out of nowhere. She was on television going into the courthouse for some such thing and I saw her and she looked so pathetic. They said that she would be represented by the public defender up in Carthage, and I saw on television it was some gal. I checked that public defender out and it turned out she was fairly new.

Then I heard that Lucy committed suicide and I almost fainted dead away. I was sick for a week and I don't think it will ever go away, the guilt that I felt that I caused all of this, that she took the fall for me when it was me who had done it.

The notebook I'd taken from Eddie's body was really just a mystery to me, just a bunch of scribbling here and there by that idiot. On one of the pages was some names, but they were almost illegible in his awful handwriting. I worked on trying to figure it out how to decipher the names and came as close as I could figure and on another piece of paper I wrote down the names and did it with my left hand instead of my right so it looked like a kid did them.

I made sure there were no prints on the paper and I drove into Carthage and knew where this public defender lived and what kind of car she drove. It was dark when I got there and I parked the car a few blocks away and walked to behind her apartment and put the notebook page under her windshield wiper. I had no idea what the names meant, but maybe they'd be clues to something connected with that kiddie porn stuff. It's the least I could do for Lucy.

Actually it wasn't the least I could do for Lucy. I could do one more thing, maybe not exactly for Lucy except indirectly, but maybe for everybody, and that was to get rid of Sherry Garand, who Eddie worked for. I figured out a plan and I think it was a good one. It took me a pretty long time to figure out what I needed to do and how to do it.

I went to his house one night when I was pretty sure he was alone and knocked on his door. He seemed a little bit surprised to see me there, but I'd worn some nice clothes and wanted to look as sexy as I could. I told him that I needed some money and would he think about hiring me back for some of his films. He laughed at me and said I was over the hill and why would I think people would want to see me in films doing what I used to do. I told him that I was hard up for the cash and that I'd do just about anything he wanted me to do. He laughed again and I said if he'd let me in I'd do a little audition to show him I hadn't lost it.

He let me in, but was still kind of laughing at me. We went into his living room and he sat in a big recliner and said go ahead, show your stuff. I started to take my coat off and was looking real sexy and I pulled a big knife from my coat and did the same to him that I had done to Eddie, pushed that thing in just about at the Adam's Apple and shoved it clear to the other side of his neck. He tried to get up but the knife pinned him to the chair and he died right away, just like Eddie did. Fuck you, Sherry, time to go to hell. I spent about ten minutes in the house and knew where he kept his files, in a safe in the basement. I knew where he usually hid the keys and there they were, right where I remembered them being. I went through the stuff in the safe and pulled out a big fat file folder. It was full of stuff I wanted to look through. Before I left the house I just looked at Sherry there in the big easy chair, his eyes were still open, the expression on his face one of shock, and his mouth was wide open and I could see all the fillings and gold caps on his teeth. I just left the house and got in my car and drove back to Keokuk.

How stupid could Garand be I thought when I got home and looked through the file. There were names, dates, financial records, the whole thing about his business, all the way back to the early days when I worked for him and even before. The next day I went to the bank and rented a safe deposit box and put the folder in there thinking it was kind of an insurance policy.

One night I drove back up to Carthage and parked my car a couple of blocks from the square and walked up in the middle of the night and threw a rock through the window of that public defender's apartment with a note attached to it. I just walked back to my car and drove away back to Hamilton.

CHAPTER 48

LARRY MAGUIRE

So here's what I did to disappear. I left my office and walked down the hallway making sure some of the other lawyers saw me leave and I told one of them I was leaving for home. I had my cash and Krugerrands in a briefcase and I walked to the bank of elevators and pressed the button to go down. But before the elevator arrived I walked to the stairway and made my way down. I was familiar with the stairway because over the years I used to walk up them when I'd come in to work in the morning. That was when I was on an exercise kick, but I recalled that once I saw a maintenance guy coming out of a doorway on the second floor of the stairway.

I walked to the second floor and found that door and it was open. It went down one floor to a big room that had a whole bunch of cleaning stuff in it, floor waxers, cleaning materials, brooms, mops, that sort of thing. There was another door way back in the room and it looked like it might be an exit. I opened it and it led to an even smaller room that had just a bunch of shit in it. I turned on the light and saw that over in a corner was another door. I opened it and the light poured in from outside. I peeked around and saw that it was one of the back alleys to the building, and probably hidden from any cameras because there were about a dozen dumpsters all around the doorway. I walked out of the Prudential Building and went down another alley until I was nearly two blocks away and then I merged into a big stream of people walking toward the subway. But I didn't get on the subway.

There was an old Goodwill store that I had passed many times over the years and I went in there and bought an old coat and hat and backpack and put them on in the shitty dressing room and transferred the money and gold into the backpack and walked out of the store, just a nobody walking down the street. It hadn't been but about four hours since that federal agent had sat in my office. I had left my cellphone at work. Larry Maguire ceased to exist. I was the guy who went out to get a gallon of milk and was never seen again.

CHAPTER 49

ANN CAMPBELL

Hancock County State's Attorney Wakefield Cole Jr., walked into Carla's office.

"I think you need to come over to the sheriff's office. A woman has turned herself in claiming she killed Eddie Crane and Sherry Garand but she wants to see the public defender before she says anything else."

"What are you talking about?"

"Her name is Ann Campbell and she said she killed both of those guys, then she just shut up," Cole said. "Let's go over there."

When they arrived at the sheriff's office Ann Campbell was sitting in an interrogation room, calmly sitting behind the table. Carla, Wakefield and Sheriff Lonny Johnson looked through the one-way mirror.

Johnson spoke: "She just walked in about an hour ago and wanted to talk with me, nobody else. She told me that she's the one who killed both of those guys over in Hamilton. She's real calm. I asked her a few questions but she said she wasn't going to say one more thing until she saw the public defender."

Carla told the two men to wait outside while she went in to talk to the woman.

"You told the sheriff you wanted to see the public defender, well, here she is," Carla said.

The woman looked up, stared at Carla. "I know who you are, I've seen you on television a couple of times."

"The sheriff said you weren't going to say anything until you talked with me. What do you want to tell me?"

"I won't talk until I know you're my attorney and we have attorney client privilege."

"I have to go out and get the state's attorney and we both can tell him that. You want to do that?"

"Yes."

Carla left the room and asked Wakefield to come in. In front of them Ann Campbell told him that Carla was now her attorney. Then Carla requested a room without a one-way mirror or microphone.

"So, now, you okay with everything?" Carla asked Ann.

"Yes."

"What do you want to tell me, Ann?"

"I'll tell you right up front I killed those two guys over in Hamilton."

"You told the sheriff that already. What evidence do you have that you actually did it, and you're not wasting our time with your confession."

"They were both killed with Columbia knives from my kitchen and I cut Eddie Crane's throat but I only shoved the other knife into Sherry right through him and into the chair he was sitting in."

Carla felt she was probably telling the truth.

"How did you know those guys?"

"I used to do porno movies for them, quite a number of years ago."

"I'm going to plead not guilty, no matter what they charge me with. I got a defense and I'm going to use it."

"What's your defense, Ann?"

"They deserved to die for what they were doing."

"That's not much of a defense if you murdered them, and that's what they'll charge you with."

"I don't care. I think a jury will be very kind with me when they know what those guys were doing."

"Juries can be harsh, too."

Ann told her the story of what happened, from the time she and Lucy worked at the battery factory up to the present time, or at least until after she had killed Sherry. Carla took notes, but didn't say anything during the narrative.

"Everything you've told me is protected, but you confessed to the sheriff that you killed those two guys, so they'll arrest and charge you with first degree murder. You know that, right? You went to their homes with the weapons, which means you intended to kill them."

Carla then spoke with the sheriff and the state's attorney. Ann was arrested on charges of murder. She was to be arraigned the next day.

Carla called Jack as soon as she was back in the office. "You're not going to believe what just happened," she said. "I think I'm going to need your help."

CHAPTER 50

ANNE CAMPBELL

The American justice system was not prepared for a defendant like Ann Campbell. Somewhere in the time between when she stabbed Sherry Garand to death and when she turned herself into the Hancock County Sheriff's Office she decided it didn't matter what happened to her, but somehow figured that her chances in front of a jury were pretty good.

It was Carla's case entirely. I offered to help and she said she wouldn't mind me sitting in court and helping her along, but she was going to be the voice for the defense. I couldn't tell what she thought of Ann Campbell's story, at least she never told me. I favored Ann, kind of admired her for her fortitude, if that's what you could call it. I kind of felt sorry for Carla because she hadn't been practicing but about three years and to come up against a case like Ann's would test the mettle of a very experienced attorney.

On the face of it the case seemed simple. It's hard to fight a confession, especially when the one making it has details about the crime that only the police know. But there was no other corroborating evidence that Ann had killed the two men. There were no witnesses, no forensic evidence to place her in either house where the crimes were committed. The police couldn't find anyone to establish that she had any animosity toward the two men, or that she had threatened them.

Ann had a fallback position that was as strong as reinforced concrete -- she didn't mind having to go to jail if she had to. The way she figured it was her life had been hard from the get-go and she could tough almost anything out. She justified the killings by saying she was removing vermin from society, and truth be known that was a pretty good tactic. Whether or not a jury would go along with her was a big gamble and as I knew already juries were capable of doing just about anything.

The whole thing was the reverse of every case I'd ever been involved with. Every one of my clients before claimed they were not guilty, at least at the start. It was a strange twist to have a client claim they did it, but had a strategy behind her actions and a fallback position that was solid as a wall of cinder blocks.

In the topsy-turvy universe of this trial if the prosecution could ask for a change of venue they should have done it. This was definitely the home-court advantage for Ann as most residents had a commonsense view of justice that harkened back to the old days. If this had happened 100 years ago Ann would be carefully hidden away and a charge would never have been leveled against her. The whole subject of the kinds of things these men were doing didn't even exist back then, or if they did things were handled secretly.

Jury selection took two days of excruciating back and forth as the legal minds of Hancock County did battle with the common horse sense minds of its residents. Some moments were even humorous when prospective jurors accidentally told the truth about their ability to remain impartial during the trial. Jack could see why a Hancock County mob in painted faces had killed Joseph Smith and his brother while they were in jail.

A jury was finally empaneled and consisted of six women and six men, pretty sensible. There was one African-American woman and one Asian woman, which was highly unusual since she might have been the only Asian in the county. Carla went for the women, the prosecution for the men. Almost all of the jurors were in a fairly tight age range from 45 to 60. About two-thirds of them had children and all of them had at least a high-school education.

Jurors always expect that once a trial starts it's going to be like a television show with everything moving along quickly. It's just the opposite, they're brought in and then everything stops as the lawyers scurry around and talk to the judge in quiet tones. It's like a play where the curtain rises and nothing happens for hours. Then the jury is dismissed for the day, told not to talk with anyone about the case. You can see the confusion on the jurors' faces as they're hustled out of the courtroom by the bailiffs. What the hell was that all about, he knew they were saying to themselves.

I was impressed by the judge, a young woman. That was going to help quite a bit because a shitty judge can make things almost impossible. She handed out instructions to the jury in terms they could easily understand and spoke to them with respect and told them how important their role was, the most important of all the characters involved inside a courtroom. I thought that was a nice touch since so many judges automatically assume they're the most important person in the courtroom.

Wakefield Cole began his opening statement and it was a good one. He was obviously pretty good at courtroom theatrics and played the part very well, better than many of the prosecutors I faced in Boston. He was old school, must have picked it up from books he'd read about courtroom drama. I could tell from the start that the jury liked him, and that would be a challenge for Carla.

Carla was a bit more nervous in her opening statement, but I thought she'd calm down as time went on. It's typical for a defense attorney to feel...well, defensive in the opening gambits of a trial. In a way it was good she showed that she was nervous because the jury can identify with being nervous, it shows that you're human, that you have some failings. Carla's size worked to her advantage too, as she looked vulnerable, little in the big chair she sat in. I sat at the defense table, too, but I tried to make myself look invisible, only looking over at the jury every once in a while.

Cole's case was simple, direct, short and I could see the jury understood every bit of it. Ann had killed the men, confessed to it and shouldn't even be on trial but should have pled guilty and be sent to prison. The only witness they presented was the sheriff who testified as to Ann's statement to him, and outlined the facts that Ann revealed details of the killings that only the killer would have known. Simple.

Carla's single witness was Ann herself. When she got up on the stand she took the oath and Carla led her through the long story of how she and Lucy had started a prostitution ring, how it led to work in porno movies, and how she came about learning that the men were involved in a child porn business. There was a whole lot of legal mumbo jumbo from the prosecution about the relevancy of this or that statement by Ann, or stuff that was only hearsay, but the jury got the point loud and clear. On cross examination Ann was completely bulletproof, you could see the frustration on Wakefield Cole's face as he tried to make Ann look bad or self-serving or evasive. She was brutally honest about herself and her background, said her piece in level tones and described every bit of how she'd gone about killing the two men. She ended her testimony not by answering a question, but by making a statement. "I killed those two men and they needed to be killed. I'll live with the consequences." She was never shrill or defensive or remorseful, her tone like she was the voice of God come to avenge what needed avenging.

She did something, too, that few defendants do – she never looked at the jury to play them for mercy or understanding. I could tell by the faces of the jury members that they felt this was just the way it was, evil needed to be stamped out. The jury understood that Ann didn't care what the hell they decided.

The closing statements by both Carla and Wakefield were good, concise, well presented but they couldn't hold a candle to Ann's testimony that was almost Biblical in its power. The judge gave the jury instructions and they were led from the room.

The jury was deadlocked after three days of deliberations. They never asked for any clarification of evidence or the law. Finally they threw their hands up and told the judge they were about evenly divided, and nobody was going to change their minds. The judge polled each juror in court and a hung jury was declared. The prosecution said they intended to re-try the case, which is standard procedure but most prosecuting attorneys never actually do. Wakefield Cole knew that another trial would result in the same outcome.

CHAPTER 51

LARRY MAGUIRE

After I left the Goodwill store with my ratty coat and stupid hat on, with a backpack on I went to a drugstore and bought a pair of sunglasses and a cane. When I got out of the store I wouldn't have been recognized by anyone who knew me. Even if I was picked up on the CCTV cameras that were everywhere it didn't matter.

I found a sleazy hotel and that wasn't easy because so much of the city was now gentrified. I got a room for the night and when I got to the room I cut up and threw away my credit cards so I'd be sure I didn't have any temptation to use them. I walked out to a McDonald's down the street and brought the dinner back to my room. It was a surreal feeling to realize that the person you'd been all your life really didn't exist anymore. I fell asleep and woke up about four in the morning. I just stayed in bed and stared up at the ceiling and thought about what my next move would be.

I wondered whether I should stay in Boston or get out of town. If I left town where would I go? There were a couple of logistical problems, one being that I needed to have prescription drugs for my high blood pressure, but I couldn't go to my drugstore, doing anything like that was evidence that I still existed. I'd have to make do without them until I could get my hands on some.

A problem I'd have is the money I had with me, and the gold coins. I had to secure that some way, couldn't be walking around with that kind of stuff in my backpack.

The next day I just roamed around the city in my new disguise. I looked like a bum and noticed that nobody paid any attention to me. I had come up with a sort of limp that explained the cane. I went to another re-sell-it shop and completed the outfit by getting some old shoes, pants and shirt, making sure that nothing matched. That evening I got some Chinese takeout and took it back to my ratty room.

That night it occurred to me that maybe I could hide in plain sight right here in Boston. Nobody had noticed me because I looked like a bum. Maybe I could even become a real bum, but one who had a lot of money stashed away somewhere that I could tap in to from time to time.

CHAPTER 52

ANN CAMPBELL

Amazingly, after the Hancock County jury couldn't decide whether Ann Campbell was guilty or innocent, the feds indicted her on a variety of federal charges, which surprised the hell out of all of us, the state's attorney included. Civil rights violations of the two victims, interstate violations of child abuse laws, and a bunch of other charges. They intended to show that Ann was actually involved in the whole operation from day one and killed the men to hide her involvement.

Ann didn't even seem upset by the ordeal that she now faced. "I don't have anything to lose and I've heard that the federal prisons are much nicer than the Illinois state prison," she told Carla and me.

She was transferred to a federal facility to await trial and I took on the case as her defense attorney. The federal prosecutors were relentless and I could never figure out why they took such particular interest in making sure that Ann Campbell would be put away for good, that the entire weight of the federal government would come down on her for what she had done. For every motion I filed they filed two countermotions and I had to get the help of two more attorneys at my firm involved, which cost a lot of money.

I had never played poker, really never had the aptitude for the game, and in some ways it intimidated me because you have to be so careful with everything you do during the game. You can't lead with your eyes, and it's almost impossible for a person to avoid giving what's called a "tell," in poker, some tiny little sign that you're bluffing.

Ann was a poker player. She smiled sometimes and I thought what does this woman know that I don't? It was as if the hand of God was behind her, that she knew that despite the fact that the U.S. government was coming down on her she had something stronger in her corner.

It turned out that she did have triple aces, in the form of the big fat file folder she'd taken from Sherry Garand's house. She asked for me to arrange a meeting with the federal prosecutors, and she wanted both Carla and me to be there, too.

What happened next was the most amazing thing I'd ever seen in all my years in law.

The prosecutors opened the meeting and did all the chest-pumping, Ann just sitting across the table from them, looking meek and mild, so small against all the suits across from her. Carla and I flanked Ann.

After the feds finished their bloviating, Ann spoke.

"After I killed Sherry Garand, I took some big files from his house and I read over them. I knew where to look for them since I'd worked for the guy," she said.

The chief prosecutor in this case stopped her, "Listen, Miss Campbell, this is highly out of line, I don't know what you're trying to do with all of this, or where it's leading, but you can stop right there."

Ann looked and him, then in a soft voice said "Can I continue now?"

What could the prosecutor say? Everyone in the room was waiting to hear what she had to tell us.

"It's a crime to blackmail anyone, and I never intended to use the files as blackmail, or as a poker chip in any legal proceedings. I put them away in a safety deposit box…"

At this point the chief prosecutor barged in. "We're going to charge you with obstruction of justice along with all the other charges."

"Well, that's fine, I guess it doesn't matter, but it can't be blackmail if I never asked for anything in return," Ann continued.

It was clear the lead prosecutor was done, and he started to rise from his chair, a look of distain on his face.

"You might want to hear me finish," Ann said quietly. The man continued to get up, indicating to his assistants that the meeting was over.

Ann continued anyway. "I had my friend get the files out and make a half dozen copies of everything. I had her send one copy to the New York Times, one to the Wall Street Journal, one to the Drudge Report, one to the Chicago Tribune, and one to the Associated Press, and one to the Hancock County Register."

That stopped the prosecutors in their tracks. They said nothing.

"I had my friend send them by certified mail three days ago and they've all been delivered. She called me and told me it's on the Drudge Report now. I never would have blackmailed anyone. I never did anything for my own benefit. The people involved in this whole operation and their customers deserve to burn in hell, and if I'm the one that helps them along, so be it."

She just continued sitting there, looking across the table. No spite, no anger, just looking at them. I'd never seen a group of feds so completely de-nutted right in front of me.

All hell broke loose that day. The names, numbers, information listed in Garand's file included a lot of shit-bums, but it also concluded the careers of some very influential people, including one federal judge, a U.S. senator, several CEOs and a roomful of lesser luminaries. Now it made sense why the feds had come down so hard on Ann.

In two days the federal charges were dropped and a small army of public relations people was working 24 hours a day trying to stem all the damage. Congressional hearings were in the offing and one of the top law enforcement officials in the government was asked to resign.

Ann walked away from all of it. In a short meeting in Carla's office back in Carthage, she summed it all up.

"From the minute I walked into the sheriff's office I did it all because of Lucy. I needed to redeem myself because she was the only real victim in all of this."

Her statement took my breath away.

Ann walked out of the office, down the corridor to the stairs and out the front door of the courthouse. We never saw her again, and somebody told us that she moved out of the county for parts unknown.

CHAPTER 53

JACK LAPOINT

Leland called me and said Sheila had called him because Larry hadn't come home the night before. Later that morning Larry hadn't shown up for some important client meetings. Leland sounded pretty upset and I told him maybe Larry went on a bender or had something going on that he couldn't tell anybody about. Truth was I was worried but didn't want to add to what sounded to me like growing panic. Larry was a guy who was always on time everywhere, just like I was.

Larry didn't show up that night, or the next day. When I got back in the office everyone was scrambling around trying to figure it out. Sheila had called the police and they found his car in the building's parking lot. There was no indication that his ATM card had been used or that he'd used his credit cards. They reviewed the surveillance tapes and there was no sign of Larry after he was seen leaving the office.

It was really upsetting and when I got to my office I noticed that there was a note on my desk with some numbers written on them. It looked like Larry's handwriting, but I couldn't be sure. What the hell was that? I called Leland and had him come in and look at the note. He said it was Larry's handwriting but he was scratching his head along with me. Then he spoke.

"It's a combination. To a safe."

We looked at each other and tried to figure this out.

"To his safe?" I asked.

"Let's see," Leland said.

We walked to Larry's office and closed the door behind ourselves. That caught the attention of some of the office staff. We closed the blinds for privacy and I knew that tongues would be wagging about that.

Leland went to the safe in Larry's closet and tried the combination. It worked and he opened the thick steel door. He pulled out an envelope.

In it were two letters, one to Sheila and one to both Leland and me:

Dear Jack and Leland:

I have so much to explain to the two of you that this letter can't begin to tell you everything. To give you an executive summary I have been working as an attorney for the Ianetta mob for the past decade. I know a lot about all the terrible things they do, including murders. They have ensured my silence by threatening to kill me. They paid me in cash and I did everything for them in secret. I'm afraid I've betrayed both of you, and the firm. It's too long an explanation for me to tell you how it all got started.

Today a guy showed up at my office who turned out to be an undercover agent for the FBI and he wanted me to flip on the Ianetta people. I'm not even sure that this guy was legitimate, or a test plant by the mob. If I went to the mob and said the Feds asked me to inform on them I'm sure they'd kill me even though I came to them first. I'm much more afraid of Sonny Ianetta and Jimmy Tracadora than I am of the feds.

I have disappeared, I haven't been murdered (at least not yet).

Please, please don't let anyone know of this note or that you know anything about me. And please give this other letter to Sheila so she knows I'm okay and not dead. Get rid of this letter and tell Sheila to tell no one (except the kids), and to make sure she gets rid of her letter.

I'm sorry for all the trouble this will cause the firm but I had to do this to save my life. I'm sure you'd do the same if you were in the same situation."

I looked at Leland and we just stared at each other. On one hand I wanted to get my hands on Larry and throttle him and then on the other I wanted to reach out and help him.

"What do you think?" Leland asked.

"I think we have to do exactly as he says," I answered.

CHAPTER 54

LARRY MAGUIRE

I realized to my amazement that by being a street person you literally disappear even though you're among big crowds all day long. Nobody pays any attention to you, you become part of a ghost army that marches around the city, or sits in doorways. Because I was walking so much every day I was getting in really good shape and losing weight. I'd let my beard grow and even I didn't recognize myself. At night I would slowly make my way back to the sleaze-bag hotel, have dinner and go to bed.

Sometimes I'd go by the Prudential Building and set up a spot to sit for an hour or two, watching everybody. One day I even saw Leland going into work and to my amazement following on his heels was Jack. I wanted to go up to them and tell them everything. I'd read in the Herald a small story about me missing and I wanted to explain what happened, that I just disappeared into thin air right in front of them.

I found out a whole lot about my fellow comrades in the ghost army of the street people. For one, they each have their home turfs, their own territories, like pigeons. They're very protective of these little spots so you have to go out on your own and stake out your own spot. Another thing I found out was that you can separate most of them into two camps – those who are truly mentally ill, and those who are just regular people who for a million different reasons fell upon hard times and never got up off the mat. Of course with the mentally ill you can't have a coherent conversation and you have to give them wide berth because you don't know what they'll do next, maybe haul off and hit you. With the others it was sort of a relaxed camaraderie, you'd come together from time to time and just talk. I found out so much about how life is like on the street. I was different, though, because I had a stash, and I had a place to stay at night. A lot of these people had no steady place, so they used shelters, or they slept in the street at night, except when it got really cold and then they had to go to the emergency shelters.

I didn't carry much money with me, maybe $20 at a time, just enough to get something to eat. The rest of my money I found a good hiding place for, somewhere nobody would ever think to look. In a way you could say I spread my money all over town, diversified it you might say. I bought a couple of rolls of duct tape and took each Krugerrand and taped it to different places all over the place, places where nobody ever bothered to look. If you notice duct tape is nearly everywhere so if anyone even came upon it accidentally it would just blend in. Whenever I needed money I'd go fetch one of them and cash it in at a different place each time. I was the gold king of the streets, although no one knew that. And gold was going for about fifteen hundred and some change an ounce. The other good thing about all of this was I was living on nearly nothing, didn't have any bills. In a strange way it was as if I was totally free for the first time in my life.

I was doing this for about a month and realized that I couldn't realistically keep it going forever. I was getting homesick.

CHAPTER 55

CORNELIUS BONOMONO

Every alarm bell went off when Larry Maguire disappeared. Jimmy Tracadora, Sonny Ianetta and everybody else were running around like chickens with their heads cut off trying to figure when the next shoe would drop.

I was one step removed from all the mess but I heard that Jimmy Tracadora had found out somewhere that the feds were trying to turn Maguire into an informant but that Maguire had disappeared on the feds, too. Smart move on Maguire's part, I figured, because Jimmy would have killed Maguire right away if he found out the feds had even approached him.

The way Sonny figured it Maguire probably had lots of documentation squirrelled away somewhere and they were determined to make a big effort to find out if he did. They hired a really good computer hacker to get into Larry's law firm's computer system and download everything. I heard they didn't find a trace in anything there that related to Sonny or the mob business. They did the same to Maguire's home computer system and there wasn't anything there, either.

But that didn't mean he hadn't written something down on paper and hid it away.

Sonny's people also did their best to find Maquire. They even had a guy who worked for them at the Prudential Building get the video tapes for the building on the week Maguire disappeared. Nothing. The guy did a great job at disappearing. He'd show up somewhere, though, make a mistake somewhere along the line.

On the other hand I figured that the feds must be just as confused as Sonny and Tracadora, unless the feds had cooked up the whole disappearance and it was really some sort of witness protection screen. But Sonny had a mole at the Justice Department office downtown and he found out from the mole that the feds were just as confused as we were.

For the time being everyone just waited and as time went on things simmered down. Maguire was gone and all was peaceful.

CHAPTER 56

BRIAN MCINTOSH

It was getting on near Christmas and Leland and I never let on that we knew anything about Larry. The police did an investigation but we just played confused and stunned and perplexed which was easy to do because we were that way. Larry's disappearance left a big hole in our firm and Leland and I were trying to do our best to have it not harm us because Larry was working on a whole bunch of cases and it's really hard to just walk into a case late in the game and take over. First of all the clients get all nervous that maybe something suspicious is happening at the firm, and even the cases that Leland and I were working on the clients were asking questions because there'd been a story in the Herald and the Globe that Larry was missing. It just raised a bunch of red flags, even though no one knew Larry had been involved with the mob. And the mob people certainly weren't talking either.

I phoned Brian and we met in his usual spot Legal Seafoods, and I explained as much as I could about Larry, and how it was affecting business at the firm.

Brian leaned back in the booth and pushed his clam chowder away, a serious look on his face.

"Jack, I don't have to tell you now that you have a problem. Let's think about this from your clients' point of view, or first from Larry's clients' point of view. You can't bullshit them in any way, you have to be upfront with them even though it's going to hurt the firm. Try to override your instinct to try and handle this or spin it. You can't and that's the mistake people make. When bad stuff like this happens you have to take your punch up front because otherwise you're going to take a half dozen punches down the road, and each one will be harder than the last."

Brian recommended that Leland and I meet with each of Larry's clients and explain as much as we could to them, and be honest with them and allow them to make arrangements with other law firms if they so wished. We told them if they stayed with the firm we'd make sure they were double-teamed with lawyers from the firm.

But we still lost almost all of Larry's clients anyway. The loss in revenues was a gut punch but we figured we'd have to just absorb that no matter what we did, it was just damn bad luck what had happened. And the clients who stayed with us weren't very pleased.

And we couldn't tell anyone what we knew, that he was probably okay.

There were rumors that Larry was seen around town, seen a couple of places out of town as well, but nothing ever came of them. He'd gone down the rabbit hole good and gone and we didn't have a clue. He sure as hell did a good job of going invisible.

CHAPTER 57

CARLA COLLINS PORTER

It was getting to be depressing around the office, what with Larry gone and every week bringing news that another client was quitting. We weren't getting any calls from new prospective clients, either, so we were stalling out. We had to let go of three really good attorneys and that broke my heart. I saw the firm go up and now I was seeing the firm go down.

The call came in about noon, my secretary said it was a Hancock County sheriff's deputy on the line. Funny, I thought, why would they need to call me?

"Mr. LaPoint, I have some bad news for you, but Carla Collins Porter was shot this morning. She's alive, but in very serious condition. We had to airlift her down to Quincy and she's in surgery now. I knew you'd want to know."

I was speechless, but not for long. My heart was beating out of control, I know the blood drained from my face.

"What happened," I asked, almost shouting.

"Well, we don't know exactly, but it appears that this guy went off the deep end and shot her outside the courthouse as she was coming to work. A guy by the name of Brandon McNear who we've had trouble with before over in Hamilton."

"She's been shot just once, in the mid-section, and they were able to stop the bleeding here at the hospital, but they wanted her down at a bigger hospital for surgery."

Jack immediately called his secretary, asked to be on the next available flight from Logan to Chicago, then a flight to Quincy and if there wasn't one scheduled tonight then a rental car. Fortunately there was a commuter flight from O'Hare to Quincy later that night and he could get in just before midnight.

CHAPTER 58

CORNELIUS BONOMONO

Jimmy Tracadora made a huge mistake, one that would cost him his life, and bring down Sonny Ianetta.

Tracadora got it into his head that he'd be a big hero if he could track down Larry Maguire and make sure the guy was never going to spill the beans on the operation. Here's how it went down. This is all guesswork but I knew how Tracadora thought and operated. He figured that who else would know more about a husband than his wife? He followed Sheila Maguire for a couple of days and found out what her movements were and when she'd most likely be home. He waited one day for her to leave and he got into her house and waited for her to come home. I guess what he figured to do was terrorize her enough that she would tell him where her husband was. At least that's what I figured that dumb psychopath would do.

She must have come home and found Tracadora there and what happened next nobody would ever know but I figured things got out of hand big time and he started to torture her. That would be his style. Then maybe he realized he'd gone too far or maybe she struggled too hard and he killed her. I read in the paper that she'd been beaten badly and strangled. I always knew that Tracadora was a savage.

Tracadora went into hiding, even from Sonny, and when the feds found out about Sheila Maguire they went ape-shit on Sonny Ianetta like there was no tomorrow. They pulled him in, pulled everybody in and pressed so many charges against everybody that the operation was at a standstill. They had cops at all our operations and harassed the shit out of anybody who was even connected with Sonny, even the Irish. The wrath of the federal god came down on us.

Sonny must have told Jimmy Olivetti to find Tracadora and kill him. It took Olivetti a couple of days to find Tracadora but there was so much heat on all of us that somebody gave him up, told Olivetti where Tracadora was holed up. He must have known that someone was going to get at him because Tracadora was ready when Olivetti tried to ambush him. They ended up killing each other in a shootout in a ratty little place near Cape Cod. I say it was a good thing they killed each other. They deserved each other.

What was even worse was that Maguire came out of hiding right after his wife was killed and he spilled everything he had on Sonny and his operation because the feds rounded up everybody and they had a witness on their side who was very motivated to put everybody away in prison. Sonny was out of business because of that murder of Sheila Maguire. They came down so hard on him that he was a broken man, like he'd all of a sudden got both Alzheimer's and Parkinson's disease. He just rocked in a chair at his house and spouted gibberish.

With me I was somewhat protected because I could work with anyone who took over for Sonny, and again I was also connected with the Irish. There was really no paperwork on me in Sonny's files, and Maguire didn't even know what I did for the mob. So I did okay during the upheaval that Tracadora caused. I didn't skip but a day or two down at the docks because of this mess and it passed us by neat and clean. Now there would be peace again, which is really what my job was, no matter who's in charge.

CHAPTER 59

JACK LAPOINT

I got to Quincy about midnight and went right to the hospital. The place was very quiet and I asked about Carla Collins Porter and the receptionist said she was on the fifth floor in the intensive care unit. When I got up to the floor it was an eerie kind of dark and I saw that there were some people in the waiting room. I walked in and saw Carla's two sons talking to a man I didn't know. It turned out to be Peter, Carla's ex-husband. We exchanged handshakes and they told me that Carla had successfully come through the surgery and that the doctors felt it went pretty well, although she had to remain in critical care for at least the next 48 hours so they could monitor her progress minute by minute.

I asked if I could see her but they told me that the nurses had requested we stay away for now, maybe the next morning we could go in and see her. She was very heavily sedated and wouldn't even know we were there, they said.

Her sons were beside themselves with worry, and even Peter was agitated, couldn't stop pacing the floor. None of us talked very much, sort of the hospital waiting-room chatter, a few sentences and then silence. I wasn't any better, worried and nervous as a cat.

I stayed at the hospital for the rest of the night and morning and had a chance to see Carla. She was wired up to about three different machines and I don't think she was quite conscious. But she was alive, thank God, and the doctor with whom I'd spoken with that morning said she was in remarkably good shape for a woman her age who had suffered a gunshot wound. Later in the morning two sheriff's deputies arrived, one from Hancock County, the other from Adams County, where Quincy is located. Carla was in no shape to talk to anyone, but they began asking us questions. They told us that Brandon McNear wasn't saying a thing, just talking nonsense to himself. The Hancock County deputy kept referring to him as Buster and then it dawned on me why the name rang a bell – wasn't that the name of one of the barflies that Lucy hung around with in Hamilton, one of the friends of Eddie Crane? I told the deputy of this connection and asked him to relay it to the sheriff, who had first checked Buster and his friend out in connection with Lucy's case. The deputy said they had already thought it was connected. The deputy also mentioned that they thought Buster may have been the person who shot Carla the first time, the .22 shot that hit her in the shoulder.

I checked into a hotel and caught a short nap and returned to the hospital about dinnertime and found that Carla had reached consciousness a few hours before and was receiving visitors. Her sons and ex-husband had been in to see her and I went in alone after they stepped out for a meal.

She didn't say much and I didn't either, but I looked at her and smiled and told her that I loved her and that she had to get better because it would be time again to get out on the river. She smiled and then closed her eyes and I figured the morphine was taking over. I stayed another ten minutes in the room and watched her sleep and then I left to go back to the waiting room. She looked so small and frail in that hospital bed, so helpless, that I broke down and cried. I couldn't recall the last time I'd cried.

The next day the sheriff called me and said they'd gotten Buster McNear to finally answer some of their questions. The sheriff said Buster was probably mentally impaired because he'd been an alcoholic for so long and he had been drunk when he shot Carla, which I figured as much. Buster had come to Carthage to seek revenge for Eddie Crane. The sheriff said the man had hamburger for brains and didn't think he'd even be able to follow a trial. In fact, the sheriff got Buster to talk by telling him that the jail was actually a mall and that if he talked he would be taken to an ice cream store, too. The sheriff had compared the .22 round they had found in Carla's car with a rifle found in Buster's apartment and the two matched – the shot that had hit Carla in the shoulder had been a first attempt by him to kill her.

Later that night after the boys and Peter had gone home I noticed a commotion in the ICU, with several nurses running back and forth. I jumped up from my chair and rushed to see what was going on. I went into the ICU and asked what was happening. One of the nurses asked me to step outside because they were busy with an emergency. I did as I was told but I could tell they were running back and forth from the room where Carla was. I watched at the window.

In about five minutes a nurse came out and told me that Carla had suffered a stroke, probably a blood clot that had gone to her brain. She said the doctor was on his way. In about ten minutes I saw the doctor rush in and then some more running around the ICU. I saw a big machine being carted in the room.

Later I found out that they have procedures and protocols for just the sort of thing that happened to Carla. They have ways of cooling down the body and mitigating the effects of a stroke, how much damage it can do. They told me that it had been only a mild to moderate stroke, and that with luck there should be little effect, but the doctor cautioned me about being too optimistic, saying these things can happen in a series when someone has suffered a trauma such as she had.

The next morning I went to the hospital early and just as I was parking my car my cell phone rang. It was Leland and he told me that Sheila Maguire had been found murdered at her home. It stopped me dead in my tracks and I had Leland slowly recount the details he knew. He'd been called by one of his contacts in the Boston Police who heard it from the Wellesley police. I walked into the hospital and went to see Carla but was hardly there at all. She was looking so much better than the day before, and the nurses said she'd had a quiet night and all seemed well.

When I returned to Boston for Sheila's funeral I found out that Larry Maguire had surfaced right away and that he was working with the feds who were furiously picking up people right and left from Sonny's mob. I'm sure the feds saw Larry as the goose who laid the golden egg. Apparently he was hidden away somewhere. I didn't stay in Boston but that day, and returned to Quincy to be with Carla.

Leland and I had a major problem on our hands. The news of Sheila's murder was the top headline – Wellesley hadn't had a murder in almost a decade. And because she was married to the disappeared attorney it made phenomenal copy in both the Herald and the Globe and all the television stations. Of course the name of LaPoint, Maguire and Stockwell was in just about every other paragraph and there were reporters waiting outside our doors at the Prudential. Almost every client had called asking to speak with either Leland or me about what was going on and how this would affect their particular case.

Brian McIntosh called me and said it was time to meet – not at Legal Sea Foods, but at his office downtown. I flew back to Boston.

When I saw him he closed the door behind us in his office and had a very serious look on his face, something I'd not seen before.

He first asked how Carla was doing and expressed his sympathy.

Then he went right to the point.

"This is what I call an existential public relations problem, Jack. Your firm isn't going to recover and the faster you realize that the better it will be for you and Leland. It will be the second or third line of your obituary, Founder of Mob Law Firm Dies."

"Close the firm as fast as you can do it, and salt the ground behind as you go," he told me. "You're not even sixty, you got many years before you. Don't spend them trying to sail a dead ship. Jump to another one and sail away."

I told Leland what Brian had told me and Leland didn't say much except that he'd think about it overnight and have an answer for me the next day.

Barney Componari called me the next day and invited me out for lunch. His advice was much like Brian's – fold the tent and go onto other things, either in Boston or elsewhere. Even my doctor called me, Howland, and told me over the phone what the two other guys had said, that there comes a time in a man's life where he has to make a decision about what kind of guy he really is, and he told me he was leaving the United States, he'd joined the group Doctors Without Borders. I wished him luck and he did the same with me.

Even Sarah Hollingsworth called and expressed her sympathy for what had happened to Sheila and Larry and to me. It was sweet of her. Barbara and Jocelyn did the same.

Everybody else I knew pretty much stayed quiet. You may know a lot of people, but when the chips are down, as they say, very few show up to support you.

When Leland and I finally talked it over closing the firm made the most sense. He was getting tired of practicing law and besides he had other things to tend to and he felt he'd made enough money to do something else that didn't require an income, or a very small one. He said maybe he'd volunteer at a free legal clinic.

We shook hands on it and within the month the firm was folded, the lease terminated and we paid all of our bills and deposited our remaining cash. The furniture was sold, and I found out from the furniture wholesaler that they have a hangar-sized warehouse full of furniture from closed-down lawyers' offices. It made me feel a little better to know we weren't the only ones to fold the tent. Besides, we'd had a great run, we were the best firm of its kind. So what if one of ours was connected with the mob?

I sublet my condo, closed up the lake house, and bid Boston goodbye.

CHAPTER 60

CARLA COLLINS PORTER

I think of my life now as two separate times – before I got shot and had a stroke – and everything before that.

I don't really recall much of the shooting. I remember crossing the street to the courthouse and a guy walking up to me and then a loud noise, I don't even know if there was any pain. The next I remember is being carried in something and looking up to the sky and seeing some faces all looking down at me. They say I was in a helicopter but I don't recall it except maybe the loud noise of an engine. They told me later that I was conscious the whole ride to Quincy, but I'm not aware of that. I was rushed into surgery, I'm told, but I didn't know any of this.

All I remember is waking up in a hospital bed and I couldn't move it hurt so much. There were machines around me and they were making a buzzing noise. I couldn't tell if there were people with me or not but I recall thinking I'm going to die if I don't get up to pee right that minute. Well of course I couldn't get up but they had taken care of the pee problem already.

Peter and the boys were at my bedside at one point but I didn't even understand what they were saying to me. I didn't even know if it was night or day. I remember a nurse taking care of me and she had a British accent and I thought that was really reassuring for some reason.

They told me I had a stroke but I don't remember any of that either. Jack was in my room and I smiled at him and then went back into my dream world which is the best way to describe it, although it wasn't quite like the dreams you have at night. I can't describe it only to say I've never had that kind of feeling before. Finally that nurse told me that I was going to be fine and that I was one tough lady. She stroked my forehead and hair and it felt so comforting.

The funny thing about this is later I asked several people who that nurse was who was from England and they just looked at me. There were no nurses at the hospital from England. I asked if any nurse worked there who was from Australia or South Africa or New Zealand, and they said no.

I couldn't use my left arm really well because of the stroke and part of my face drooped but they said that may go away in time. I had trouble trying to come up with the right word when I was talking with people. I knew the right words but my mouth wouldn't pronounce them right. It was very frustrating.

I remember the day Jack took me back home to Carthage and I was so glad to be back in my own bed. He took such good care of me and I told him about the British nurse and the fact that nobody at the hospital said there was any such person. Jack said strange things happen and maybe we don't know much about another world that exists alongside of ours. He said maybe that when I was really bad off I went into that parallel world and she was from there.

There were a lot of things that seemed so strange during the time I was getting better. I had an unexplainable craving for tapioca pudding. Jack was forever going out looking for it. That lasted for about a month, then it just ended and I never wanted to look at another tapioca pudding in my life. Also, I was always ready for sex, craved it just like I did tapioca pudding. Jack was trying to keep up with me and after about a month it was just like the pudding, I didn't want any more.

One night I fell into a deep sleep, so deep it even worried me because I thought maybe I was dying. I had a dream and that nurse was there in my room. She didn't say anything and I tried to ask her questions but she didn't answer, she just held a little baby in her arms, a beautiful little girl with golden hair.

I got better and Jack was a big help, my boys too, they were always around. Eventually I was ready to go back to work but I had to take it easy and I worked only half-days. I took work home and after Jack made me dinner I worked from my bed on the cases that were piling up. Jack tried his best but he's really an awful cook so we had a lot of take-out. Jack would stay over a lot although he had his own apartment and many nights he slept in the other bedroom because he said I needed my sleep and he'd disturb me with all his tossing and turning.

CHAPER 61

CORNELIUS BONOMONO

After all the shit died down and things got back to some semblance of order I got a call one day from Sal Galvini, a guy I've known for years. He was always a go-to guy who was like a lieutenant in command of Sonny's operation. He asked me to go to lunch with him up in New Hampshire where he had a summer home.

It was a long lunch and there were a number of other guys there, most of who I knew. They had a proposal for me, they wanted me to be the temporary head of the operation in Boston. They only wanted me there one year until they could decide which guy was going to take over for good. They said I was the perfect one to be a transition because I had a reputation for being level-headed and fair, and because I was the guy who worked with the Irish organization. They said I could have free rein to do what I thought right, just don't do anything too rash and if I wanted to make any big changes to check with them first.

I told them that I did want to make a change and said I wanted to get rid of some of the hotheads we had in the organization, some of the stupid shits who Sonny had around all the time. They said okay, and asked me to give them a list of who I thought should be removed from the organization, and they'd go through it.

Mary and my kids knew nothing about any of this, of course. I didn't even change where I worked, just kept my little office near the harbor. But I was running everything from that little place. My intention was to clean up the whole operation and give to the next guy a very clean office. I know my dad would have been very proud of me, running the whole deal.

One thing I missed was having lunch with Jack. I was very sorry about what happened to his firm but it couldn't be helped, Maguire had ruined it for everybody. Maguire and that psychopath Tracadora. But I knew that Jack was alright, he'd gone back to where he came from and was with a woman he adored. Maybe someday when Mary and I had some time we'd go out to see where he lived.

CHAPTER 62

LUCY WETTERAU

They didn't treat me nice at all when they arrested me at Eddie's house that morning. I was naked from my waist down and they just left me there like that, all of them looking at me. Finally a woman cop came in and yelled at the other cops to let me put some underwear on and some pants. Thank God she was there otherwise I think they were just going to take me outside naked for all the neighbors to see.

They put me in handcuffs and drove me in the backseat of a police car over to Carthage where they did a whole lot of things to me like take a picture of me, get fingerprints, take samples of some of Eddie's blood on me, get a saliva sample from me. At the jail I got cleaned up and they even looked up my rectum and vagina and in my mouth and they took some of my own blood. They had read me my rights at Eddie's but it was just a blur. I didn't even know what I was saying to anybody.

They put me in a little room and asked me questions for what seemed like hours. I said I wanted to see a lawyer and this skinny woman showed up and told the cops the questions would stop right there. They did. Then she talked with me – I told her that before she got to be my lawyer I wanted to make a call to a man I once knew – Jack LaPoint. I told her he was a lawyer in Boston and would she mind finding a phone number for him so I could call him. She said fine and then told me not to say anything to the cops or anyone else without a lawyer being there.

I got in touch with Jack and his voice was the best thing to hear. I was out of my mind with fear and he calmed me down, I remember thinking he sounded just like he did so long ago. He told me the same thing that woman said, don't talk with anyone. Jack said he'd help.

The next two or three days were a huge blur to me, I was going into withdrawal from everything I was using and my mind was barely working. I even thought there was somebody in my cell with me but there really wasn't. I was vomiting and sweating and once I even wet myself and shit all over my pants. In jail you go cold turkey, it's not a rehab center. Thank God there were a couple of nice guards who helped me out, I think they were kind of used to this happening and they knew what to do.

A lawyer from Quincy came up and said that Jack had sent him and he asked me a bunch of questions but I was fucked up and I don't even know what I told him.

Then Jack arrived to see me and oh my God I hadn't seen him in so many years. I was so excited to see him and he looked just like I remember him. I wanted to hug him and kiss him, but I couldn't because they made him stand behind a big yellow line outside my cell. I looked like shit but he just smiled and I could tell that he was glad to see me. He asked me a few questions and then left. I cried all night.

I wish I could explain all of my crazy thinking for the time I was in jail. I'd stay up almost all night looking out this little window at the top of the wall in my cell and I wouldn't move a muscle, just stay motionless.

Jack and that other woman lawyer came to ask me a lot of questions and I had a hard time trying to remember some of the things that happened that night at Eddie's house. A lot of it was a mystery to me, but I know I didn't kill Eddie. In a way I started to think it really didn't matter to me either way whether I killed him or not. I started to lose interest in a lot of things and I was thinking over what I'd done with my life, how useless I was, and what did anything matter anyway? I thought about that little baby of mine and thought what would have happened if she had lived and now I'd have a grown daughter and she'd be pretty like I used to be. After a while I quit crying and couldn't start back up crying no matter how sorry I felt about things.

CHAPTER 63

CARTHAGE

It turned out that Carla's recuperation took more than a year. The wound healed nicely and she had no trouble there, but the stroke had done some permanent damage, not enough for most people to notice, but I could. She wasn't as sharp as she'd been before, and every once in a while she couldn't find the right word to express herself. But I was amazed at how far she'd come from when I saw her in that bed in the hospital, just a little thing with all the machines hooked up to her.

I drove Carla home when she got released from the hospital. I stayed at her apartment for about two weeks to help her with everything, then I found an apartment for myself which was just off the square but light years away from hers in opulence. When Leland and I closed the firm I got a pretty good slug of money that was still in our reserves and with what I'd stashed away in the safety deposit box I'd be fine for years if I watched my expenditures, probably fine until I died. I had put both my Boston condominium and lake house up for sale. I was shocked at how little my living expenses were in Carthage, hardly anything at all.

I took care of Carla for the first couple of months she was home, visiting with her every day and doing her errands and helping her out with the various therapies that she was undergoing. She tried to go back to work too soon and collapsed on the courtroom floor. They called 911 and back she went to the hospital for a couple of days but just for observation. She was fine, just trying to do too much too quickly, the doctors said.

I was still licensed to practice in Illinois and I went around to the half-dozen other attorneys in town and asked if they needed help. I got no takers so I thought about starting my own practice and I finally went and did it, renting an old house just off Main Street and hanging out my shingle. For two weeks the phone didn't ring, then a young couple came in and asked if they could make out a will. I was off and running. I charged them $250.

Carla was getting stronger and I was spending a lot of time at her condominium, mainly to be with her but the added benefit was it was so much nicer than where

I lived. The reason I got my apartment was I never wanted Carla to presume that I was just going to move in with her. If that's what she wanted, fine, but I'd let her make that decision, not me. After six months she hadn't asked me to move in, and that was fine with me. I slept over there most of the week anyway.

Buster never went to trial, the judge having agreed with the sheriff that the guy had hamburger for brains, so they put him away in a hospital and said he'd only live a year or two, that's how much damage the alcoholism had done.

I got to know Carla's friends and we had a good time having dinners together and bumming around Hancock County, and, of course, going on the river. I'd bought a boat and trailer and kept it behind my apartment.

Carla finally went back to work and was strong enough to put in eight hours a day. I could tell just small effects from the stroke and I don't think most people realized that she'd ever even had one.

Leland got in touch with me to say that he and his boyfriend were getting married and would Carla and I come to the ceremony. We were delighted and flew to Boston to attend, a wonderful service downtown. Late into the reception, after Leland and I had too much to drink, we huddled together and talked about the firm and both of us started crying. We had no idea what had happened to Larry, and figured he was in some sort of witness protection program.

Leland asked me how it felt being back to the place where I'd been born and raised. I told him that sometimes it was like the thirty-something years I'd been gone were just a bunch of chapters in a book and the last chapter ends in the same place where the first chapter began. I think he understood what I was talking about but we were both pretty drunk.

I flew to Boston several times to tie up loose ends and I called Cornelius Bonomono and asked him if he'd like to have lunch. We met down near the harbor at the restaurant we always went to. It turned out his son was working with a law firm in New York City, one of about 150 attorneys and working day and night and earning so much money he didn't know what to do with it, and didn't even have time to spend it. We never once talked about business, so we didn't break that tradition. He and Mary were thinking about calling it quits pretty soon and enjoying their two grandchildren, maybe in a year or so. He said he may even want to leave Boston and get away from all the stress.

I checked in with Brian and told him how my life was shaping up. Naturally we met at Legal Seafoods and he made me pay the bill, as usual. Like Cornelius, he was thinking of throttling back, maybe even selling his firm to one of his long-time competitors who he hated, but who had asked him if he wanted to sell. He wanted to write a novel and said that he'd like to come out to Carthage, drive up to where Edgar Lee Masters was from. He also wanted to go down to Hannibal and see where Mark Twain was from. What he wanted to do was take a long driving trip through the United States, stopping at the homes of famous writers.

They buried Lucy out in Rock Spring Cemetery which is about a half mile from Carthage, out in the country, a really pretty place, and I went out to see her grave. My parents are buried there, too, and I made sure to go over and see their graves. Lucy's tombstone was so small I almost missed it. I said a little prayer for her and that night I had a dream that I was out on the river and I had found something, but the dream ended before I could find out what it was. In the dream I remember pulling on a rope and looking down at my arms and chest and belly and I was lean and strong.

Made in the USA
Coppell, TX
01 March 2020

16332092R00118